Vindicated
Book 6 in the Jenny Watkins Mystery Series

1. Driven
2. Betrayed
3. Shattered
4. Exposed
5. Trapped

Hi Marcia,

I hope you enjoy this one! Enjoy reading it by the pool, that is; not that I'm jealous or anything.

Love, Bud

Copyright 2014

Dedication

I want to thank my family, Scott, Hannah, Seneca, Evan and Julia for their continued support. I couldn't do any of this without you.

Bill Demarest is the world's best fact checker. Some of the content in here is against his better judgment, but I figured my readers wouldn't mind a few truth-stretches. ☺

Danielle Bon Tempo is the grammar guru. How is it my 'finished product' gets returned to me with a sticky note on every other page? Thanks for finding the things I didn't!

This one also goes out to Colleen Krezel, who hosted a book club about Driven and invited me. My first book club…that's something to remember.

Lastly, my thanks goes out to you, my readers, for encouraging me to follow my dream. You all ROCK!

I hope you all enjoy Vindicated!

Chapter 1

Jenny placed her hand on her tiny baby bump and smiled as she read the document in her hand. Biting her lip, she headed into the kitchen. "Hey," she said casually to Zack, who sat at the table. "I just got something interesting in the mail."

"Oh yeah? What is that?"

She held up the paper. "I'm officially divorced."

A huge smile graced Zack's face as he got up from his seat. "Really?" He slid his hand around her waist. "That's great."

She hugged him in return. Releasing the embrace, she asked, "Is sex with me still going to be as exciting now that we're no longer having a torrid affair?"

"I'm not sure," he remarked with a smirk. "I think we should go find out."

Jenny let out a hearty laugh and kissed him on the cheek. "You know, I may be the first pregnant woman in history that's happy to receive divorce papers."

He thought about that notion for a moment. "You know, somehow I doubt it. *But,*" he added emphatically, "I do have something to give you." He disappeared into the bedroom that he shared with Jenny.

She chewed on her fingernail as she awaited his return; somehow she felt nervous, even though she knew what was coming. Zack did indeed come back into the kitchen with the little black box he had presented to her three months earlier, opening it to reveal the ring that Jenny had been eager to wear since her acceptance a week later. "I believe this belongs to you, m'lady," he said as he lowered down to one knee. "And now that you are *officially single*, you can wear it proudly." Glancing up to her with a smile, he slid the ring on her finger.

She looked down at her hand, admiring the way the modest solitaire diamond looked on her finger. Her gaze drifted beyond her hand to the clearly-delighted face of the man she loved, invoking an even deeper sense of happiness. She placed her hands on Zack's cheeks, gently guiding him to stand up so she could give him a kiss. "Actually, I believe I'm *officially engaged,* thank you very much."

"Ah, yes," he replied playfully. "Sorry, I won't make that mistake again. So...do you want to make the call to find out when we'll become *officially married*?"

Without a word Jenny smiled and picked up her phone, remembering the agreement she and Zack had made a few weeks before. A woman answered in a professional tone. "Fairfield County Government Center."

"Hi," Jenny began. "I was wondering if I could schedule an appointment to...get married." The words sounded surreal as she said them.

"Sure," the woman replied happily, "when would you like to come in?"

"What's your first available date?"

"Let me see," she said slowly, as if she was reading a screen as she spoke. "The judge has an opening at two o'clock tomorrow."

"That sounds great." Jenny glanced at Zack, giving him the thumbs up and mouthing the word *tomorrow*. "Although, we don't have our marriage license yet. I am under the impression that there's no waiting period on that?"

"That's correct," the woman clarified. "You'll just need to come in early to the clerk's office with your social security cards and driver's licenses. Then, once you get your marriage license, you can go to the judge's chambers and have your ceremony. You can bring in up to six guests and dress however you'd like."

"That sounds fantastic."

"Okay, can I just have your names and I'll schedule the appointment?"

"Yes. I'm Jennifer Watkins, and my fiancée is Zack Larrabee." She could hear the keystrokes in the background.

"Well, first let me offer my congratulations," the woman said cheerfully, "and we'll see you tomorrow at two."

Jenny knocked on the door to the basement, from where her mother, Isabelle, called, "Come on down."

At the bottom of the stairs, Jenny found her mother watching television in the living room of the in-law suite she called home. "Hi, ma." Waving her left hand in the air, she added in a sing-songy tone, "Look what I got."

Isabelle's face lit up. "Oh, honey, that's great. I guess that means the papers came."

Jenny took a seat on her mother's couch. "They sure did." Bracing herself for the conversation she knew she was starting, she continued, "And I just got off the phone with the folks at the courthouse. It looks like I will be single for precisely one day."

The pleasure left Isabelle's face, and her shoulders drooped. "One day? Really, Jenny?"

Jenny had expected that reaction, and her mother didn't disappoint. "I know it seems like I'm rushing into this, but Zack and I have actually been engaged for a few months; I just haven't been able to wear the ring because the divorce process takes so long." She softened her tone and her expression, knowing her mother only had her best interests at heart. "The reality is, we want to get married as soon as possible for the sake of this baby. I'm already four months pregnant, and eventually this child is going to be able to do the math. We want to put as much separation between the wedding and the delivery as possible."

Isabelle, too, sounded more compassionate. "But is the courthouse really the way to go? Are you *sure* you don't want to do something a little...fancier?"

"I'm sure, ma." She smiled lovingly at her mother. "Believe it or not, that's actually a good thing. The last time, when I married Greg, I was so excited about being a bride that I didn't give enough consideration to what being a wife was going to be like. And, yes, I had an amazing wedding day, thanks to you." It was not lost on Jenny that her parents had spent a small fortune sealing a union that didn't last. "But then after the honeymoon, I came home to a life that didn't make me happy.

"This time is going to be different," Jenny continued. "I like my life now. I don't need a big, extravagant ceremony to make me happy. I'm perfectly content with what I already have." She patted her mother's hand. "We'd just like to make it official for the sake of the baby."

"I know," Isabelle acknowledged. "You've said all that before. I just want to make sure you won't look back at this and regret it. I don't want you to feel cheated out of a beautiful ceremony."

"I've already had one of those," Jenny said.

"But Zack hasn't. How do you know he won't feel slighted?"

"Because he's Zack," Jenny said flatly. "Trust me, he won't feel like he's missing out on anything."

"Are you *sure*?"

"Positive." Jenny replied. "In fact, a ceremony would probably only call attention to the fact that he's not on the best terms with his family. His parents don't even know about me...or the baby."

Isabelle shook her head with disapproval. "I can't imagine that," she uttered, even though she was already aware of the situation.

"I've told you about his father," Jenny continued. "His dad takes every possible opportunity to remind Zack that he's a screw-up. I can't blame Zack for not wanting to tell his father that he'd impregnated somebody else's wife. But after we get married..." A sly smile appeared on Jenny's face. "We plan to go down to Georgia so he can introduce everybody to *his* pregnant wife. His father will have a much harder time finding fault with that."

"You don't think he's going to criticize Zack for keeping him in the dark about it?"

"Zack hasn't spoken to his parents since before we moved to Tennessee. It's not like they've been chatting and he's simply failed to mention it. They've had a falling out." Jenny shrugged with cautious optimism. "We're thinking that maybe this baby can serve as an olive branch."

"I just have a difficult time imagining that a family can go that long without talking." Isabelle looked upset. "It doesn't seem right."

"Well, not all families are as close as ours." She raised an eyebrow at her mother. "But even our family has a few skeletons in the closet."

Pursing her lips, Isabelle demonstrated defeat. Turning the conversation back to a place where she knew she had a leg to stand on, she added, "But aren't you going to want your brothers there when you get married? Or Rod? Or Ingunn?"

"Sure, it'd be great to have them all there," Jenny said, "but I'm allowed exactly six guests in the courtroom. Which six people would I choose? And if people are coming in from out of state, suddenly this wedding becomes a much more formal affair, which is exactly the kind of thing we're trying to avoid." She placed her hand on her mother's arm. "Trust me, ma. I'm happier this way. You're the only wedding guest we need."

Isabelle digested the words, glancing down toward her lap. With renewed vigor she sat up straight and said, "Okay, that's fine...but will you at least promise me that you'll get your hair done?"

Jenny sat with her hair in an up-do, complete with a few loose curls framing her face. She had opted for a pale pink dress with an A-line cut to hide her baby bump; somehow she didn't find white—or form-fitting—to be an appropriate choice.

Zack, who wore a Hawaiian shirt and khaki pants, glanced at Jenny out of the corner of his eye. "You look great, you know."

"Thanks," Jenny whispered with a smile. She held on to her single rose—the 'bouquet' she acquired at the insistence of her mother—and waited anxiously for their names to be called. Isabelle dabbed at her eyes with a tissue. "Are you okay, ma?"

"Yeah, I'm okay." She flashed a weak smile. "It's just that my little girl is getting married, you know?"

Jenny wondered if those were tears of pure happiness or if her mother was also mourning the absence of her husband of forty years, who had passed away just six months earlier. Out of fear of getting tearful herself, Jenny decided against focusing on her father at that moment. She didn't want sadness to cloud what should have been a joyous occasion.

Mercifully, the judge opened the door and greeted them. "Miss Watkins and Mr. Larrabee?"

Jenny drew a deep breath before she stood. "That's us," she announced, taking Zack by the hand and walking through the door of the judge's chambers. It boggled her mind that when she walked back out through those doors, she'd be doing so as Zack's wife.

Zack's wife.

The judge was younger than Jenny had anticipated, and he wore a smile that, most likely, few people ever saw while he wore that robe. "I hear you two are here to get married."

"That's the rumor," Zack replied as he shook the judge's extended hand.

"I must admit this is one of the more pleasant aspects of my job," the judge said as he shook Jenny's hand as well. He inspected the marriage license and asked if Zack and Jenny had more guests than just Isabelle.

"No, we don't." Jenny felt unpopular.

"Well, we need two witnesses, so let me just get a clerk in here." He disappeared for a moment, returning with another employee of the courts, who seemed genuinely happy for the couple.

Circling around behind his desk, the judge pulled a folder out of his drawer. "So, did you two write your own vows?"

Jenny grimaced apologetically. "Were we supposed to?"

The judge shook his head. "No, not necessarily. It's just an option if you want it." He looked back and forth between the couple and added, "I guess I'll just go with the traditional ceremony, then?"

She smiled with relief. "That sounds perfect."

He pulled a piece of paper out of the folder and returned to the front of the desk, telling the couple where to stand and giving them a brief description of what was about to transpire. Jenny's nerves tingled as she handed the rose to her mother and took Zack's hands in hers. She looked up into his eyes and flashed a nervous smile, which he returned. This was it. This was the moment they would become husband and wife—the moment they would remember forever.

She could hardly believe it was happening.

The judge began. "Today we will be celebrating in the union of Jennifer Lynn Watkins and Zachary Ryan Larrabee. Are you, Jennifer, here under your own free will with the intent to marry Zachary?"

Looking squarely at Zack and positively brimming with love, she whispered, "I am."

Are you, Zachary, here under your own free will with the intent to marry Jennifer?"

He gave Jenny's hand a subtle squeeze. "I am."

A million little memories flooded Jenny's mind as she looked at Zack's face—the face she'd laughed with and struggled with—the face that had greeted her in the mornings and comforted her during her darkest hours. This was now going to be the face of her *husband*—the face she would turn to for decades to come...the face that would eventually become wrinkled with age but would always welcome her home at the end of the day. "Do you, Jennifer, take this man to be your lawfully wedded husband, to love him and comfort him, honor and keep him, forsaking all others, as long as you both shall live?"

She was so choked up she could barely speak. Eventually, she managed a weak, "I do."

"Do you, Zachary, take this woman to be your lawfully wedded wife, to love her and comfort her, honor and keep her, forsaking all others, as long as you both shall live?"

Zack's smile reflected a mixture of love and happiness. "I do."

The judge turned his attention to Jenny. "Jennifer, please repeat after me."

She stated the vows, her voice cracking with emotion. "I, Jennifer, take you Zachary, to be my lawfully wedded husband, to have and to hold, for richer or for poorer, in sickness and in health, as long as we both shall live." A tear worked its way down her cheek.

Zack's face was the most serious she'd ever seen as he took his turn reciting the vows. "I, Zachary, take you Jennifer, to be my lawfully wedded wife, to have and to hold, for richer or for poorer, in sickness and in health, as long as we both shall live." The gravity of the situation was almost overpowering to Jenny. She bit her lip and sniffed as another tear escaped her eyes.

The judge turned to Isabelle and softly asked, "Do you have the rings?"

In a merciful moment of levity, Isabelle searched frantically for a way to free up her hands. She passed Jenny's rose off to the clerk before producing the rings, handing them over to the judge.

He held up the overlapping rings for a moment, proclaiming, "These rings are a token of your love and fidelity; may they forever serve as a reminder of the promises you made here today."

He handed Zack's ring to Jenny, who in turn slid it on his finger, repeating the judge's words, "With this ring, I thee wed."

Wed. She had just officially pledged her life to Zack.

She held out her hand as Zack took his turn putting the ring on her finger. She heard his voice crack subtly as he said, "With this ring, I thee wed."

And now he, too, had just pledged his life to her.

The smile on the judge's face was broad. "Well, then, with the power vested in me by the state of Tennessee, I now pronounce you husband and wife." Holding out his hands wide, he added, "You may kiss the bride."

Jenny looked lovingly into Zack's eyes, and for the first time she kissed her husband.

Chapter 2

"What time are they expecting us?" Jenny asked, referring to Zack's family.

"Well, they're expecting *me* at seven-thirty," he explained. "They still don't know about you yet."

Jenny gripped the steering wheel as she stifled a laugh. "Is this going to be explosive?"

"Explosive? No." Zack grinned evilly as he looked over at Jenny. "But it *is* going to be funny as hell."

"Humor is in the eye of the beholder. I'm not entirely convinced that I'm going to be laughing while these events unfold."

"Oh, I will be," Zack said with confidence. "My father is going to shit his pants."

Jenny glanced at the clock as she shifted in her seat, trying to head off the tingling that threatened her backside. "I feel like we've been on the road forever, and we still have forty-five minutes left."

"We're in the homestretch, look at it that way."

A stir began in Jenny's stomach. She reached over and turned off the radio, giving her the ability to concentrate fully on the pull she was beginning to feel. Applying the turn signal, she maneuvered into the right-hand lane of the highway, trying desperately to get over in time to make the quickly-approaching exit.

Zack said nothing as they made their unexpected detour. He was used to her psychic insight prompting her to make unforeseen turns; this was why she always did the driving.

She had driven for only about five minutes after exiting the highway when she pulled the car into a residential neighborhood full of average-sized houses of varying styles. After a few lefts and rights, she turned onto a long street that ended in a cul-de-sac. At the very end of that road, she parked along the curved edge of the circle and turned the key.

Emerging from the car, she approached a split-foyer home situated at the end of the street. She walked a few steps up the driveway and froze as she stared intensely at the house. Flashes appeared before her eyes like photographs. A bloody woman lying on the floor with horror gripping her face. A knife on the carpet. A coffee table overturned from a terrible struggle.

She turned to Zack, who had approached silently and stood by her side as she absorbed the message. Pointing to the house she whispered, "Somebody died in there."

Zack placed his hand on his wife's back and posed, "And they're contacting you?"

Jenny shook her head. "No, the victim isn't contacting me." She glanced over at him. "The killer is."

"Holy shit," he replied. "That's a new one."

She clasped her hands together in front of her mouth as she considered her options. "It looks like the people who live here are home. The garage door is open and there's a car in there. Do you think they will let me come inside?"

Zack shrugged. "It's worth a shot."

With Zack a few paces behind, Jenny climbed up the steps in front of the house and rang the doorbell. She heard eager footsteps bounding toward the door; she was greeted by a young girl about eight years old with long blond hair fastened back in a messy ponytail. A second, slightly taller girl appeared behind her.

"Hi," Jenny said in the voice she'd often used in her classroom. "Is your mom or dad home?"

The younger girl didn't bother to say anything more to Jenny and Zack; she simply yelled, "Daaaad!" and walked away from the door.

She had left the door open just enough for Jenny to see the girls' father appear at the top of the steps in a wheelchair. He climbed out of the chair, standing unstably on his legs, which were clad with metal braces. He slowly worked his way down the six stairs that led to the front door. Jenny felt horrible for making him go through so much trouble.

He finally appeared at the door and said, "Hi, can I help you?"

Jenny wrung her hands and twisted her face before beginning in a tone that indicated she knew she sounded strange, "Hi, my name is Jenny Watkins, and this is my boyfriend Zack." She realized her mistake immediately. Last week Zack was her boyfriend; today he was her husband. Undeterred, she continued. "And I know this is going to sound bizarre, but I'm a psychic, and I just felt a really strong pull to your house. I get the feeling that..." Jenny was unsure how to continue considering she didn't know if the murder had impacted this man personally. Eventually she said, "...something bad happened here."

He nodded unsentimentally. "Yes, a woman was killed here back in the eighties." He kept the door open but used the banister to lower himself into a seated position on the stairs. Once situated, he continued, "But that was before we moved here."

Jenny felt relief. "Do you have any affiliation with the victim?"

The man shook his head. "Nope. I just happen to live in the same house."

With a smile, Jenny said, "Well, that makes things easier to discuss, then."

He furrowed his brow but kept his tone pleasant. "What's to discuss? The case was solved within hours." He pointed his hand in the direction of the house next door. "It was open and shut—the neighbor's kid did it."

"Well, I get the impression the neighbor's kid is trying to tell me something." At that moment Jenny's own words occurred to her. "Wait a minute...*kid*? Just how old was this murderer?"

"Eighteen, I believe."

"Eighteen?" Jenny shook her head with disbelief. "What on earth could possess someone so young to do something so horrible?"

The man shrugged. "I'm not sure what his motive was."

She paused, glancing at the house next door. Neighbors. How differently their lives would have unfolded if just one of them had decided to buy a different home. "Does the family still live there?"

The man once again shook his head. "Nah. From what I understand they moved pretty quickly after that, and I can't say I blame them."

Jenny imagined the torment that family must have endured after the murder. Justified or not, the hate they must have felt from the people in the community would have been unbearable to live with.

Despite her wandering mind, Jenny couldn't deny the spirit's pull was still strong; she wanted to be inside the house. She did her best to appear friendly, smiling brightly and talking in a chipper tone. "Listen, Mr....Oh, I'm sorry, I don't even know your name."

"Rob Denton."

"Mr. Denton, for some reason I feel the need to be inside your house. I think the killer is trying to tell me something, and being inside would give be a better reading."

Understandably, he looked skeptical. "No offense or anything, but I'm not sure I want to let a couple of strangers inside my house."

"I completely get that," Jenny said sympathetically as she opened her purse. Fishing around inside, she pulled out one of the business cards Zack had given her for Christmas, handing it over to Rob. "I'd like to invite you to investigate me. If you search the Internet, you'll find several examples of my psychic ability solving criminal cases." She smiled genuinely. "I promise, the only reason I want to be in the house is because it was the scene of a murder many years ago."

Rob carefully inspected the card, which had Jenny's name but Zack's contact information. "I'm guessing you're Zack?"

"Yes, sir. The one and only." Zack flashed a cheesy pose.

After more contemplation, Rob called up the stairs. "Brianna, can you bring me my tablet please?" Soon the little blond girl reappeared, handing Rob the device before scampering back up the stairs. Jenny stood patiently as he did his research.

Eventually, Rob looked up at them with a shrug. "I guess you're legit. Why don't you come on in?"

Rob stood up by using the banister to pull himself upright. With much effort, he twisted his body to position his braced legs on the first stair, repeating the process as he worked his way up to the top.

Jenny wasn't sure of the politically correct thing to do, but she spoke anyway. "Would you like me to give you a hand?"

"Nah," Rob said in a tone that implied he didn't take offense, "I've been doing this for five years now."

Zack and Jenny waited patiently as Rob worked his way up the steps, eventually lowering his body into the wheelchair he had left at the top. As Jenny climbed the last step, a wave of familiarity came over her, causing her to close her eyes to absorb the image. She stood frozen for a moment before opening her eyes and looking back and forth between the two men.

Zack could recognize the look on her face. "What is it?"

She sighed as she gathered her thoughts. "The person who is contacting me had apparently come up this way." She gestured to the steps she'd just climbed. "And as he reached the top of the stairs, he saw the victim lying on the floor."

Looking confused, Zack posed, "If you saw the vision through the killer's eyes, what was the victim doing already lying on the floor?"

Jenny shook her head. "Apparently, I'm not being contacted by the killer. I'm being contacted by a witness or a paramedic or something, because the woman had already been attacked by the time I saw her. Based on the amount of blood I'm seeing, I'm guessing she'd been stabbed or shot." She looked up at Zack. "Multiple times."

"She *was* stabbed," Rob confirmed. "I think it was something like seven or eight times."

With a subtle nod, Jenny acknowledged his comment. "But she was alive when this person got there. She was lying over here," she remarked, moving to a spot on the floor in front of the coffee table. Pointing toward the opening to the kitchen, she added, "Her head was this way, and she was curled in a fetal position. She looked terrified, and she was reaching toward me. I was definitely not a threatening presence; she was looking for my help."

"So, you don't know who you were in the vision?" Zack asked.

"I have no idea," she replied, "but the person obviously witnessed the crime, or at least the aftermath of it."

Zack raised an eyebrow at her. "And in order for you to get contacted, that person must also be dead."

Jenny thanked Rob for his cooperation—and his phone number—before she and Zack headed out to her car. As soon as their seatbelts were buckled, Zack was on his phone looking up information about the murder. "Okay," he said out loud, "the town is called Mumford Springs, according to my GPS. Let me check this out." After a pause he continued. "Just as I suspected…it wasn't hard to find. I don't think Mumford Springs is a real hotbed for murder, so this incident is the only one that came up when I searched it."

"What does it say?"

Zack skimmed the article on his phone. "Apparently it happened back in 1988. The victim was a twenty-six-year-old nurse named Stella Jorgenson. She rented the house with Megan Casey, another nurse who was twenty-seven and wasn't home when the murder happened. The guy was right…the neighbor who was convicted was eighteen; his name was Nate Minnick."

Jenny remained silent as she digested the information. Everyone involved was so young; the notion was mindboggling.

"It seems another neighbor heard a commotion and went outside in time to see Nate running from the house, covered in blood with a knife in his hand. Nate ran into his own house and closed the door behind him. The witness went into Stella's place to find her lying there with stab wounds and called the police."

"That must be the person who is contacting me. Did it say the name of the witness?"

"Willy Sanders."

"Willy Sanders," she repeated softly, wondering exactly what this Willy Sanders wanted.

"Apparently, the police brought Nate in to the station, where he confessed." Zack continued, raising his eyes to look at Jenny, "Once again, it appears Rob was right...the case was open and shut."

Jenny processed the information. "I'm reluctant to believe it could be that easy if this Willy Sanders guy is bothering to contact me about it. Something about this must be upsetting him if it's made his spirit linger for nearly three decades."

"Could he just have been disturbed by what he saw?" Zack posed. "I know I would be forever scarred by the image of a neighbor with eight stab wounds."

Jenny shrugged. "At this point I can't say."

The car was quiet for a short while before Zack remarked, "Do you know what other image will scar me for a while?"

"No, what's that?"

"The image of Rob struggling to go up and down those steps."

Jenny nodded subtly. "Yeah, that was a little tough to watch."

"Let me see something," Zack said as he continued to play with his phone. He pressed a series of buttons before announcing, "Just as I thought. Rob has owned the house for ten years."

Jenny was confused. "Why does that matter?"

"Well, he said he'd been going up and down the steps like that for five years now. He apparently was involved in some kind of accident—he wasn't born like that. But this was the house that he lived in before the accident, and he must have wanted to stay for some reason."

"He may have something degenerative," Jenny suggested, "and the braces weren't necessary until five years ago."

Zack shook his head. "I doubt it's degenerative. If he knew he'd ultimately lose the use of his legs, he wouldn't have bought a house with so many steps. I bet he had no idea this was coming."

Jenny gripped the steering wheel a little tighter, realizing that every day people get behind the wheel to make casual trips, only to have their lives forever changed by a single moment of carelessness—sometimes someone else's carelessness. "You're probably right," she replied. "He must not have known."

"And did you see what I saw on the floor?" Zack asked.

"I saw a dying woman," Jenny remarked dryly. "What did you see?"

"Carpet." He threw his hands in the air. "Plush carpet, no less. How is Rob supposed to get around in a wheelchair on carpet?"

"It can't be easy," Jenny agreed.

"I wonder why he hasn't renovated or moved."

"If I had to guess?" Jenny said. "Money."

Zack remained quiet for a moment before he said, "We have money."

"Yes, we do have money." Jenny didn't look at Zack, but she smiled at his comment.

"And I have some skill," he added.

"As does your whole family, who lives just forty minutes away."

"I don't know; it's June. Larrabee Construction might be overwhelmed right now. Remember, most people want to move in the summer, so this is a terribly busy month for the guys in the field."

Jenny shrugged. "Well, you still have skill."

"I *do* have skill." He seemed to be thinking as he spoke. "I can certainly rip up some carpet and lay down some hardwood, and a ramp wouldn't be that hard to build."

Making a face, Jenny asked, "A ramp? Wouldn't that be a little steep?"

While he clearly found the comment amusing, Zack refrained from laughing. "I don't mean a ramp inside; I mean *outside,* to make those front steps easier. I was thinking we could install one of those chairlifts on the inside."

"Can you do that?"

"No, but we can hire some people to do that." Quickly he added, "That is, if you're okay with it."

"Oh, I'm okay with it. I'd love to see life get easier for him."

"Good," Zack said with a vigorous nod for emphasis. He folded his arms over his chest and remarked with a smirk, "And by the way, I'm your husband, not your boyfriend."

Jenny's nerves fluttered as they pulled into the Larrabee's driveway. "Are you *sure* this isn't going to be a problem?"

"No, it's not a problem," Zack assured her. They got out of the car and shut the doors. "I've gotten married and I'm going to be a father. This is something I've finally done right."

"But we got married a few days ago. I obviously got pregnant a few months ago."

They proceeded up the walkway that led to the front steps. "But I manned up. My father's got to respect that, at least."

She sucked in a deep breath as Zack opened the unlocked front door. "Honey, I'm home!" he called.

"Yeah, and you're about forty-five minutes late," a male voice grumbled from around the corner. Jenny surmised that had to have been Zack's impossible-to-please father. As expected, an older man walked into sight, but he stopped in his tracks when he got a look at Jenny. He furrowed his brow with confusion and asked, "So, who do we have here?"

"This is Jenny," Zack said with obvious pleasure in his voice. "She's my wife."

Chapter 3

"She's *what*?" Zack's father posed with disbelief.

Before Zack had the chance to answer, his mother appeared in the hallway, immediately wearing a look of pleasant surprise. "Oh! I didn't know you'd be bringing a friend."

"That's not his friend, that's his wife," Zack's father said a little too loudly.

Jenny hadn't exhaled since they'd walked through the door.

"Zack?" Mrs. Larrabee looked back and forth between the couple. "Is this true?"

"Yes, mom, it's true."

She walked over to Zack and Jenny, reaching out and grabbing each of their left hands. Noting that they were wearing matching rings, she looked at her son and exclaimed, "Why didn't you tell me?"

Zack shrugged. "I've been busy." The gratification had left his voice when he spoke to his mother. Jenny knew that the lapse in his relationship with her had been collateral damage in his attempt to alienate his father.

"You've been busy," Mrs. Larrabee repeated without contempt as she hugged Zack and kissed his cheek. "You've been ignoring my phone calls; that's what you've been doing." She turned to Jenny and placed her hands on her shoulders. "And what is your name?"

Jenny said her name nervously, unsure how these people felt about her presence.

"Well, Jenny, I'm Ellen. It's very nice to meet you. I'm sorry that my goofball son has kept us in the dark about your existence. I'm sure this has to be a very awkward moment for you."

Jenny smiled pleasantly. "No, it's okay." She was lying through her teeth; this was the most awkward moment of her life.

"That's polite of you to say," Ellen replied with a sly smile, "but I know you're full of it. But by all means, come on in." She playfully smacked Zack on the back of his head as he walked by, mentioning, "I guess you won't be sleeping in the twin bed I made up for you."

"I can sleep on the couch," Zack said. "No big deal."

Jenny noted that Zack's father still stood in the same spot, looking disapprovingly at his son. Now was the time for a little bit of redemption on her husband's behalf. She wore her friendliest smile as she approached him and extended her hand. "Hello, Mr. Larrabee. I'm sorry we were late; it was my fault. We were on our way here and I got a contact, so we had to take a little detour."

He lowered his eyebrows. "A contact?"

"Yes, sir, a contact." She bit her lip and added, "It's probably best if I explain it to both you and Ellen at the same time."

"So, how long have you known each other?" Ellen asked as they sat in the living room. Zack's parents each sat in a recliner; the younger couple sat on the couch.

"We met last summer," Zack replied. He turned to Jenny. "What was it, August?"

Jenny nodded with a smile.

"And when did you get married?" Ellen still seemed shocked.

"Just a few days ago," Zack said.

"And you didn't *tell me*? Why on earth would you have gotten married and not told me?"

"We kept it small," Zack replied.

"You kept it small," Ellen muttered. "There's small, and then there's secretive."

Zack shrugged. "Okay, we kept it a secret."

"But, why?"

Jenny was grateful that Zack was doing the talking.

"I could tell you," he said, "but then I'd have to kill you."

Apparently used to her son's antics, Ellen just shook her head. "Can you at least tell me how you *met* without having to kill me?"

"He helped me with a case," Jenny explained. "My first case, actually, where I had no idea what I was doing." She patted Zack's leg lovingly. "I don't know what I would have done without him. He was absolutely instrumental in getting it solved."

She noted Mr. Larrabee looked stunned at the prospect that Zack had actually accomplished something worthwhile. His expression only increased Jenny's desire to rave about him.

"Case," Ellen said. "What do you mean by case?"

Jenny told the story of how she discovered she had psychic ability when she was contacted by a spirit who had ties to the Larrabee family.

Zack chimed in, "Dad, do you remember when I asked you for pictures of Arthur? That was so I could help her."

Zack's father only grumbled in return.

Jenny's smile in Zack's direction exuded pride. "When I was working on that case, I was having a lot of marital trouble. My husband—at the time—wasn't being very nice to me, and Zack here reminded me what it felt like to be treated with respect. Actually," Jenny added, turning her attention to Zack's parents, "*remind* is the wrong word. No one has ever treated me as well as Zack has, so I guess I should say he *showed* me what it was like to be treated well."

While Ellen looked pleasantly surprised, Zack's father demanded, "Zack, did you pay this woman to come here and say these things?"

"Andy, don't be rude," Ellen reprimanded with disgust. Turning to Jenny she softly added, "Don't pay any attention to him. I, personally, am delighted to hear Zack is so good to you. I will admit I did worry about him a little bit, afraid that he still had too much growing up to do, but it sounds like he's turned out okay."

"Yes, ma'am, he's turned out just fine." She turned to Zack's father, still sporting her smile. "And I assure you he didn't pay me to say these things. I sincerely mean them."

Andy looked at Jenny skeptically but didn't say anything.

"Well," Zack interjected, "I guess it's time to bring up one more little thing."

"Here it is," Andy said, looking at Ellen. "He wants money."

Jenny felt both anger and disappointment toward Andy. It seems Zack hadn't been exaggerating when he'd talked about his father's poor opinion of him.

Ellen, too, seemed to share in Jenny's sentiment. She looked as if she was going to give Andy a good tongue lashing as soon as they found themselves alone. She made a dismissive gesture toward him, turning to Zack and saying, "What is it, honey?"

Zack put his arm around Jenny. "We're due to have a baby on November eighteenth."

Ellen's jaw dropped. "A baby? You're going to have a *baby*?"

Jenny smiled and nodded.

Ellen got up from her seat and walked over to the couch, cupping Jenny's face in her hands. "Oh my goodness." She kissed Jenny on the cheek. "Did you hear that, Andy? They're going to have a *baby*." She moved on and kissed Zack's cheek as well.

"Yeah, I heard," Andy said, clearly far less impressed with the news than his wife. He shook his head and said, "Babies are expensive, you know. Are you sure you're going to be able to afford this?"

Zack's patience was obviously running out. "Dad, we're fine. Money is not a problem."

"Last I checked you don't have a job."

Zack looked like he was ready to blow, so Jenny jumped in quickly. "Oh, he does. He is my partner in my psychic business, and the income is...substantial."

"Psychic *business*?"

"Yes," Jenny replied, remaining calm, "we've turned my ability into a business. When spirits contact me, we find out what it is they want, letting their living loved ones know."

Andy still didn't seem impressed. "And people pay for that?"

"Well, we've actually only had one paying customer—Elanor Whitby. That first case—the one that brought Zack and me together—involved figuring out what happened to her missing boyfriend. As you probably know, Miss Elanor passed away last year; what you may not know is that she left me the bulk of her estate. That inheritance alone resulted in eight figures." Jenny took great pleasure in making that statement, although she kept her tone matter-of-fact.

Andy appeared as if he was searching for a way to put a negative spin on her words, but he was unable to do so. "Eight figures, huh?"

"Yes, sir." Jenny interlaced her fingers. "Without decimal points."

Zack and Jenny got undressed in the guest room, which Ellen had quickly prepared since it had a queen bed. "I swear to God, I hate that man," Zack said. "Now do you see why I haven't spoken to him in months?"

Jenny patted his arm lovingly. "Yeah, I get it. I'm sorry, honey."

"It's not your fault the man's an asshole."

"But your mother seems nice," she replied, hoping that would be a consolation.

"My mom is great," Zack said. "And so is my sister. It's my dad and my brother that drive me up a fucking wall."

"Would you rather stay in a hotel?"

Zack didn't reply; he only shook his head as he turned down the covers. The image of Zack looking so defeated made Jenny sad.

"If it makes you feel any better, I think your father is doing a lot of thinking right now...trying to figure out how his *screw-up son* turned out to be a husband and a father and a multi-millionaire." Jenny climbed into bed, realizing at that moment just how tired she had been.

"Yeah," Zack scoffed, "and I'm sure he'll find a way to make me look like an asshole by morning."

Jenny leaned over and kissed his cheek. "Well, you should keep doing what you're doing and be the bigger man. You know what they say...living well is the best revenge. You don't need to get into a shouting match with him; let your success speak for itself."

"That's a good theory," Zack noted, "but I make no promises."

Jenny nestled into the bed as Zack turned off the light. Her brain threatened to be her own worst enemy again, as it immediately conjured up the horrible image of Stella Jorgenson suffering from her stab wounds on the floor of Rob Denton's house. There she was again, looking at Jenny, reaching out her bloody hand in a desperate cry for help.

This time, however, Jenny paid attention to the one little detail she had overlooked before. She immediately sat up in bed, reaching over and turning on her lamp.

"What's up?" Zack asked, looking over his shoulder.

"I was just thinking about the Jorgenson case." Jenny shook her head subtly. "I think we have it all wrong."

Chapter 4

"What do you mean *we have it all wrong*?"

"Can you call up that article again?" Jenny asked. "The one you read in the car?"

Zack reached over and grabbed his phone, clicking the same links that had led him to the article the first time. "What do you want to know?"

"The knife," Jenny said. "Correct me if I'm wrong, but Willy Sanders said he saw the murderer running out of the house with the knife in his hand."

Zack skimmed the article. "That's what it says."

"Well, when I played the vision in my head one more time, I distinctly saw the bloody knife on the floor a few feet away from Stella." She turned to Zack. "How could Willy Sanders have seen the neighbor's kid running out of the house with the knife in his hand, only to go inside the house and see the knife still there?"

He thought for a moment. "Two knives?"

"Have you ever heard of a murderer using two knives?"

"Two killers?"

Jenny considered the notion. "Maybe. Either way, something is up." With the wheels turning in her head, she asked, "Is there any way we can see if Mr. Willy Sanders is still alive?"

"I'm not sure. Give me a minute." Jenny waited patiently as Zack did his research. Eventually he added, "According to the white pages, he is very much alive and still lives in the house next door."

Jenny looked at Zack with wide eyes. "Okay, so it appears he's not the one contacting me after all. But then who could it be? Who else had been in that house?"

"The neighbor kid was," he noted. "The one who confessed to killing her."

"What was his name again?"

"Nate Minnick."

She scratched her head and repeated his name in a whisper. "What was his sentence? Did the article say?"

After a little bit of reading, Zack announced, "Life without parole."

"Okay, let's see. If Nate was eighteen when the murder happened in 1988, that means he was born in 1970...which means he would be in his forties now. And if he's been in jail this whole time, unless he was murdered in prison, he would have had to have died of natural causes." She glanced at Zack. "Isn't forty-something a little young for that to happen?"

"It is," he reasoned, "but it's not out of the question. Even children can die of natural causes."

Jenny placed her hand on her belly and pretended she hadn't heard that. "Can you find out if Nate is still alive?"

"I can try." Zack spent the next fifteen minutes searching sites on his phone, only to concede, "I'm sorry, but I can't find anything."

"That's okay," she replied. During Zack's search, fatigue had really crept into Jenny's bones; she yawned before asking, "Does it say which prison he went to?"

"Enon State Prison."

"I'll call them in the morning. Do you think they'd tell me personal information about one of their inmates?"

"I have no idea," Zack said. "Are they bound by confidentiality?"

Jenny didn't know the answer to that. "Forget it. I'll just call Kyle Buchanan in the morning; he'll be able to figure it out easily, I'm sure."

"Is that the world's best private investigator?" Zack asked.

"The one and only." Jenny's eyes got as bright as her level of exhaustion would allow. "Hey...we're in Evansdale. I can actually *go in to his office and see him* instead of just calling him."

Zack let out a little laugh. "You seem awfully excited about that. Is he hot or something?"

"No, he's not." Jenny conjured his image in her head, recalling that he was a slightly-overweight and disheveled middle-aged man. She spoke with emphasis. "Not at all. It'll just be great to see him in person considering how many times he's helped me."

Zack stretched with a loud groan. "So, is that the plan for tomorrow?"

"I think so," Jenny replied as she turned out the light. "That, and contacting the folks at the chairlift store."

Kyle Buchanan stood up with a smile from behind his messy desk. "Jenny Watkins. How great to see you again." He extended his hand, which Jenny eagerly shook.

"It's nice to see you, too." She didn't bother to correct him regarding her name.

He gestured for her to have a seat, and she obliged. "So, is this a social call, or do you have more business for me?"

Jenny blinked repeatedly, emulating southern charm. "Why, I do have some work for you, if you have the time."

"You're a very generous tipper," Kyle noted with a wink. "Therefore, I always have time for you."

"And that is why you are the world's greatest private investigator," she replied with a laugh. "I was actually wondering if you could tell me if a man named Nate Minnick is still alive."

He flashed her a strange look. "I assume you'd like his contact information?"

"No," she replied, shaking her head. "I just want to know if he's alive."

"That is quite an unusual request." Kyle leaned forward on his elbows with a playful smile. "What, exactly, is it you do with all this information I give you, Ms. Watkins?"

"I'm not sure you'd believe me if I told you," she replied with an equally playful look.

He leaned back in his chair. "Well, I think I can honor this request easily enough. Do you happen to have a last known address of this Mr. Minnick?"

"I do. Enon State Prison."

"That's maximum security," Kyle noted.

"I'm aware."

After a short visual standoff, he remarked, "At least that should make it easier to find out his information. I can have an answer for you this afternoon, most likely."

"Great." Jenny stood up and put her purse over her shoulder. "I guess I'll let you go so you can get started. Oh, and let me pay you now. Do you think one hour will cover it?"

"It should," Kyle said. "I'll let you know if it's longer."

Jenny reached into her purse and handed him four hundred dollars in cash. "There's your regular rate, plus a little tip for you."

He shook his head. "You scare me a little, Ms. Watkins. How do you always have so much money to throw around?"

She opened her purse again and pulled out one of her business cards. "Here," she said, placing the card on his desk. "This may answer both of your questions in one shot."

"I'm nervous," Jenny declared as the car rolled to a stop in front of Rob's house. "Suppose he's insulted by the offer."

"I know, I've had the same thought," Zack replied, "but hopefully he'll understand it's rooted in good intentions."

"I guess to be safe I should try to get the reading first, just in case he kicks us out."

The couple got out of the car and approached the house. Zack lowered his voice to a near whisper and said, "See, I'm thinking the ramp can go out a little bit and then turn toward the driveway." He outlined the path with his hand. "There are only five steps in front of the house, so the angle won't be too steep, even though the distance is short."

Jenny could picture Zack's description, and the thought of Rob being able to get around more easily warmed her heart.

Since their visit was expected this time, Rob didn't come to the front door. His daughter let them in and Rob met them at the top of the stairs. "How are you guys doing today?" he asked casually.

"We're okay," Jenny said. "Thanks for letting us come back. I'm getting the impression that I misinterpreted some things last time I was here, and I'm hoping to clear that up."

"That's fine," Rob said kindly. "Y'all are just lucky I work from home; otherwise you'd be coming to an empty house."

"What do you do?" Zack asked.

"I'm a database administrator for the county government. I have to run a lot of reports and manage security clearances, but it's nothing I can't do from here."

Zack's face reflected his approval. "That's not a bad gig."

"It saves us a bundle on daycare, that's for sure."

"Okay, I hate to ask this of you, but is there any way I can be in the living room alone for a few minutes?" Jenny asked. "Since I'm not feeling a pull this time, I'm going to need to focus if I stand a chance at getting a reading."

"That's fine," Rob said. "I have work to do anyway. Zack, do you want to come with me? You can hide out in my office. If my daughters get their hooks in you, you'll get roped into playing Barbies."

Zack smiled and gave Jenny one last look of encouragement before following Rob down the hall.

Jenny took a deep breath and rolled her shoulders before descending the first two stairs toward the front door. She stopped and turned around, facing the area where Stella had once lay dying. With her body relaxed and her eyes closed, she was eventually able to see an image of the room as it had looked twenty-five years earlier.

A floral couch sat along the wall, and the overturned coffee table in front of it indicated a struggle had taken place. The dark brown carpet was plush and hid the blood stains well, although Jenny was sure there must have been a pool around Stella—she was far too bloody for there not to be a mess on the carpet. She had the same look of horror on her face as she did in the previous vision, and she once again reached out, positively desperate for help.

Jenny noted the knife on the ground a few feet from the victim. "Miss Stella," she heard herself say in a deep, male voice. She ran toward the bloody woman, stopping for a moment to pick up the knife and look at it, trying to grasp what had happened. With the knife still in hand, Jenny knelt at Stella's side; her knees became blood-soaked from the invisible puddle on the carpet. Stella grabbed Jenny's shirt with both hands, covering it with blood. Even more blood spurted from a wound in Stella's abdomen, soaking the bottom part of Jenny's shirt.

Stella looked as if she wanted to say something.

A loud bang, presumably from the girls playing in the basement, caused the vision to disappear instantly. Jenny stood still for a moment, absorbing the implications of what she'd just witnessed. It appeared that not one, but two injustices had occurred back in 1988, and while she could do nothing to stop one, she knew she was being tasked with rectifying the other.

Jenny walked down the hall, which was covered with framed photographs of people Jenny assumed to be the Denton's family and friends. Although she ordinarily would have enjoyed looking at those, she ignored the images, focusing instead on finding Zack and Rob. They were in one of the bedrooms, which had been converted into an office.

"Did you have any luck?" Zack asked when she entered the room.

Feeling sad, Jenny nodded slowly.

"What did you find out?"

"It turns out I didn't need Kyle Buchanan's help after all. This vision definitely came from Nate Minnick, the young kid next door."

"So he *is* dead," Zack said as more of a statement than a question.

"Yes. He's dead and he's innocent."

"What?" Rob asked with dismay.

Jenny let out a deep exhale. "He didn't do it. He stumbled across Stella after she'd already been stabbed."

Zack looked solemn. "But what about him running from the scene with the knife? And the confession?"

"The confession I don't know about," Jenny said, "but I distinctly saw him rush into the room when he saw Stella bleeding on the floor. He picked up the knife and looked at it with confusion; I could sense that he had a difficult time processing what was going on. But then he turned his attention to helping Stella, and he forgot he had the knife in his hand. I imagine he took the knife with him when he ran out of the house."

"Where was he going? Why didn't he call 9-1-1 from Stella's house?" Zack asked.

Jenny shook her head. "Panic, I guess? I'm not sure. He was just a kid, remember. But according to Willy Sanders, Nate ran out of Stella's place—covered in blood and carrying a knife—and went back into his own house. That was perceived as him fleeing the scene, when in reality it was a huge misconception." She pointed her finger in Rob's direction. "Speaking of Willy Sanders, I'm under the impression he still lives next door."

"He does," Rob replied.

"Can you tell me a little bit about him?" Jenny asked. "Would he have made a reliable witness?"

The sincerity in Rob's voice was remarkable. "Willy Sanders is one of the nicest people you could ever meet. He would never have done anything to throw off an investigation. If he said he saw that kid running out of the house with a knife in his hand, then he saw that kid running out of the house with a knife in his hand."

Jenny smiled. "You sound positive about that."

"There's not a doubt in my mind."

"Okay, so I guess Nate ran out of the house and took the knife with him." She shrugged her shoulders. "But I still know he didn't do it."

"Then why did he confess?" Zack asked.

Once again, Jenny shook her head. "I can't answer that."

"Well," Zack said, "I guess now we know why his spirit lingers."

Jenny nodded sadly. "He wants to be exonerated."

"What strikes me," Rob began, "is that if this kid didn't do it, then the person who committed a murder in this very house is still on the loose."

After a long moment of silence, Zack clapped his hands together and said, "Well, then, let's see what we can do to change that."

Rob leaned back in his chair and smiled. "Well, feel free to come by the house again if you need to. I have to admit, I find this whole thing fascinating."

"Thanks," Jenny replied. "We just might take you up on that." Trying to choke down her nerves she added, "But we were actually thinking we might offer you up a little service."

Rob looked curious. "What's that?"

"Well," Jenny began, "let me start out by saying that Zack and I do this business because I was left a large inheritance by my first client, with the stipulation that I use the money to do good things for people. As you probably can guess, we won't get paid for clearing Nate Minnick's name—we're just doing it so his soul can be put at ease." She cleared her throat nervously. "But sometimes we do other nice things with the money...for instance, we paid for treatment for a guy with addiction issues, and Zack fixed up his house so he could sell it for a profit once he got out of rehab." Jenny hated the uncertainty in her voice; she wished she could have been speaking confidently. "And, um, the last time we were here, we did notice that your house isn't exactly conducive to life in a wheelchair...and we were wondering if you would allow us to make some adjustments to it to make your life a little easier."

Rob's face remained blank, leading Jenny to wonder if she'd overstepped her bounds. Eventually, he simply said, "What kind of adjustments?"

"Well, I have a few ideas," Zack began, "if you wouldn't mind following me so I can show you."

Zack and Rob toured the house while Jenny tagged along, Zack pointing out all of the changes he'd make. Besides the chairlift and the hardwood floors, he also suggested enlarging the door openings and making modifications to the kitchen, where the current island made maneuvering the wheelchair difficult. He mentioned redesigning the master bathroom to include an accessible shower, as well as putting in a larger, lower mirror and a pedestal sink.

"You can do all of this?" Rob asked.

"I used to work construction before this job. Have you ever heard of Larrabee Homes?"

Rob shot a skeptical glance in Zack's direction. "Yeah, I've heard of them. They make all of those mansions, don't they?"

"Yup," Zack replied, "and my name is Zack Larrabee."

"Okay," Rob said, shaking his head as if to make sense of the situation, "if you do make all of those fixes, do you know how much that's going to cost? The chairlift alone will be a couple thousand; we've looked into that already."

"It's really not an issue," Jenny said. "Consider it a payment for letting us use your house for readings."

Rob's expression slowly grew into a smile. "I swear I must have a guardian angel or something. Ever since the accident, I have been convinced that someone's watching out for me up there, and now two complete strangers have just rung my doorbell and offered to modify my house for me." He finally looked like he was on board with the idea. "This is just amazing."

"Do you mind if I ask what happened in the accident?" Zack asked. While Jenny had been thinking it, she didn't have the courage to bring it up the way Zack just did.

"No, not at all. It was a car accident. I was driving on the highway late one night, and I fell asleep at the wheel. The car drifted off the road and hit a tree." He once again shook his head, appearing to marvel at his luck. "When I consider how many ways this thing could have unfolded, I realize how fortunate I am that I didn't kill anybody, including myself. I was going about sixty-five miles an hour. You should have seen the car. It's a miracle that I even survived."

Jenny smiled, acknowledging that Rob must have been a very kind-hearted man. She imagined that many people in his shoes would have felt victimized, but he considered himself lucky. He was definitely a glass-half-full kind of guy.

"I did receive a spinal cord injury, but it was incomplete."

"What does that mean?" Jenny asked.

"It means it didn't fully paralyze me. I still have some use of my legs, although it is limited. I use the wheelchair because it's easier and I can get around faster. I've got two kids that go a million miles an hour; I can't afford to be slow."

Jenny giggled. "No, I imagine you can't."

Zack chimed in, "I assume this was your house before the accident and you didn't want to move?"

"Exactly. Didn't want to move. Couldn't afford to move. Didn't have time to think about it. You name it. For the sake of the girls, we wanted to stay put—they'd been through enough by just watching their father suffer—they didn't need to pack up and move to a new home. But we also had a ton of medical bills that the insurance didn't fully cover. We ended up taking out a second mortgage on the house, and we used that money to pay off the medical bills and buy an adapted van so I can still drive. We figured we'd eventually make the house more livable for me, but so far we haven't been able to find the money."

"Well," Jenny said with a smile, "thanks to Elanor Whitby, now you have."

While Zack and Rob started to make plans for the renovation, Jenny snuck out to the neighbor's house, hoping she could get the chance to talk to Willy Sanders. She rang the doorbell several times, but nobody came to the door. From the porch, she spun around and looked at Rob's house, noting the relatively small yards had given Willy a good vantage point on the day of the murder. If his character was as solid as Rob suggested it was, there would have been no question about what had transpired that day.

After venturing back to Rob's, Jenny discovered the men were still talking logistics; she found herself wishing she had driven separately. Quickly bored by discussions of hardwood and kitchen layouts, she walked down the hall and looked at the myriad of framed photographs on the wall. She recognized some of the people as being the Dentons, but still other people looked as if they were unrelated. An older, African-American couple graced a lot of the shots; based on their frequency, she imagined they were among the Denton's best friends.

Jenny smiled as she looked as the pictures; this family seemed to value the people in their lives, which added to the affinity she felt for them.

Once she had examined every picture twice, she walked out into the living room and took a seat on the couch. While she wasn't having another vision, she did picture Stella lying on the floor, looking helpless and terrified. The look on her face implied that she knew she was going to die. Jenny shuddered at the thought.

Her phone rang, causing her to jump. Looking at the caller, she saw it was Kyle Buchanan, the man whose morning she'd just wasted.

"He's dead," Jenny said instead of hello. "I figured that out. I should have called you and let you know to stop looking."

"Wow," he replied, "that was quite an unexpected greeting." His voice sounded pleasant. "What gave it away?"

"If I tell you, you probably won't believe me."

"Try me. It can't be any worse than the bomb you laid on me this morning, my psychic friend."

Jenny snickered with defeat. "I saw a vision, and based on the facts of the case, I know it had to have been through Nate's eyes. I'd only be able to see that if Nate is dead."

"What, exactly, did you see?"

Her tone reflected her sadness. "I saw evidence that he didn't murder his neighbor, which was what he went to jail for." Jenny explained the story to Kyle, who hung on her every word. "It seems he's contacting me so I can clear his name, although I do wish he was alive so he could enjoy his freedom once I do...if I do."

"Well, it turns out he wasn't incarcerated very long," Kyle noted. "He died back in 1991, after only three years in jail."

"What?" Jenny exclaimed with disbelief. "He was only twenty-one years old then."

"I know. It's crazy."

"What did he die of, do you know?"

"According to the coroner's report, it was a heart attack."

"A heart attack?" Jenny couldn't believe it. "At twenty-one?"

"It seems he had a congenital heart defect. Sadly, a long and prosperous life was not in the cards for this young man."

The happiness that Jenny had felt for Rob just a few moments earlier was gone, replaced instead by an overwhelming sense of melancholy. How could life have been so unfair to some people? "Mr.

Buchanan," Jenny began, "I want you to do a few more things for me, if you don't mind."

"I'm actually not very busy right now, so I'd appreciate the work. What is it you have in mind?"

"Well, I was wondering if you could look into the details of Stella Jorgenson's murder. If the wrong guy went to jail, that means her killer is still roaming the street."

"I can do that, sure."

"And another thing," Jenny continued, "I'm wondering if you'd be able to find Nate Minnick's parents…"

Chapter 5

Jenny sat across the kitchen table from Ellen while Zack was at the home improvement store. With Andy at work, Ellen was able to speak freely. "I'm sorry you have to witness the bickering between Zack and his father." She shook her head and pursed her lips. "I'm used to it by now, but it must be very uncomfortable for you."

After taking a sip of water, Jenny said, "Well, I will admit Zack warned me about it, so I had plenty of advanced notice."

Ellen seemed to ignore her comment. "I swear, I don't know what it is with those two. They've been going at it for decades, and if you ask each of them, they'll say it's the other's fault."

"It's really been like this for *decades*?"

Ellen nodded emphatically. "Ever since Zack was a child." She let out a little chuckle as she recalled a memory. "He was always the kind of kid who did the opposite of what everybody said. If Andy said left, Zack went right—and boy did it ever infuriate Andy. Disproportionately so, I think. And then of course he'd yell at Zack—who, in turn, made doubly sure to defy his father the next time. It's been a downward spiral ever since."

Jenny looked at her sympathetically. "It must drive you crazy."

"It does, and I hate the fact that it made me miss your wedding."

Suddenly, Jenny felt selfish. "Well, if it makes you feel any better, everybody missed our wedding. We got married in a judge's chambers in the county courthouse." She bit her lip. "We needed to have a court employee be our witness."

"Why so small?" Ellen asked without judgment. "Didn't you want your family there?"

Jenny shrugged. "My mom was there." If she could have sucked those words back in, she would have. "But she lives with us," she added quickly, hoping that explained why her mom was present but Ellen wasn't.

"She lives with you?"

"Well, kind of. She lives in the basement apartment." Jenny repositioned herself as she began the explanation. "My father died recently...well, the man who raised me did." She held up her hands to start over. "I have two fathers—the one who created me and the one who raised me. It's a long story, but the man who raised me died recently, and my mother was struggling to live in their house alone. The memories of him haunted her. Then I found out I was pregnant, which threatened to pose a problem, logistically speaking. I often feel pulls at random times, and I have to just drop everything and go where they take me. Obviously, I can't leave a baby home alone while I follow the direction of a spirit."

"Couldn't Zack stay home with the baby?"

"He could," Jenny replied, "but he likes to accompany me on those trips, especially at night. He feels it isn't safe for me to venture out in the middle of the night alone."

"And I agree with him," Ellen said in a maternal tone.

"So," Jenny continued, "we figured my mother could move into the basement apartment—that would solve both problems at once. Well, three problems, actually. My mother got out of the house that contained all the memories of my father; I have a permanent babysitter living right in my home, and my brother and his family moved into my mom's old house. He had been renting, and the landlord had told him he needed to find a new place to live without a whole lot of notice." Jenny smiled. "It actually worked out perfectly for everybody."

"It sounds like it did," Ellen agreed, "but I'm sorry to hear about your father."

Jenny lowered her eyes. "Thanks."

"What about the other man—the one who created you. Are you in contact with him?"

"I am now. Honestly, I didn't even know he existed until recently. It turns out he also has psychic ability—it runs in his family—so there's a chance you might end up with a psychic grandchild."

Ellen looked impressed. "Now, wouldn't that be something?"

At that moment Zack walked through the front door with a look of accomplishment on his face.

"Check you out," Jenny exclaimed as he approached. "This looks promising."

Zack's walk was more of a dance as he sauntered down the hall. "I just submitted some plans to the county for the ramp in the front of the house, *and* I have a shipment of hardwood flooring arriving at Rob's place sometime tomorrow between ten and two."

"Wow, you're on fire," Jenny remarked. "But here's a question…how do you plan to single-handedly put in an entire house worth's of hardwood flooring and build a handicapped ramp and widen doorways and remove a kitchen island and remodel a bathroom in a matter of days?"

"The answer is: I don't." Zack touched the tip of Jenny's nose before reaching down and giving her a kiss. "I've summoned the help of some of Larrabee Custom Home's finest reject contractors."

Jenny furrowed her brow. "What exactly constitutes a *fine reject contractor*?"

Zack sat at the table with Jenny and Ellen. "Someone who does perfectly acceptable work but my father fired because he's too damn finicky."

"Zachary Ryan," Ellen scolded, "stop talking like that about your father."

"Sorry," Zack said, turning back to Jenny. "He's too *darn* finicky."

"Honestly," Ellen muttered as she shook her head. Jenny felt badly for Zack's mom.

Zack continued without batting an eye. "I've got a decent floor guy lined up, and a drywall guy named Bill can make the doorways bigger."

Ellen raised an eyebrow at her son. "Why don't you just ask your father to help you? He's more than qualified, and I'm sure he'd enjoy doing some charitable work."

"So he can constantly tell me that I'm doing everything wrong? No, thank you. I'll stick with the land of misfit contractors."

Jenny's phone rang, mercifully, and she excused herself to take the call. Just as she had hoped, it was Kyle Buchanan.

"Hello," she said with optimism. "Were you able to find anything?"

"I was. I have the Minnick's contact information for you. They live about an hour from Evansdale."

"That sounds great." She glanced at Zack and Ellen, adding, "I wouldn't mind taking a little road trip right about now."

Jenny rang the doorbell of the Minnick's modest house. Nate's father had seemed pleasant over the phone, but Jenny was still nervous about the meeting. She was never quite sure what to expect when she showed up at people's houses.

The door opened to reveal a friendly-looking, white-haired man with a beard. He bore a slight resemblance to Santa Claus; Jenny took comfort in the likeness. "Mr. Minnick? I'm Jenny Watkins, we spoke on the phone."

She was Jenny Larrabee. One of these days she'd remember that.

"Yes, hello Jenny. Please, come in. And call me Alex."

She stepped through the threshold into the living room, where she introduced herself to Nate's mother, Kim, who also appeared friendly but clearly struggled to get around, most likely due to age. Her steps were small and required obvious effort.

Once the trio was situated in the living room and formalities exchanged, Jenny explained the purpose of her visit. With a sigh she began, "As I explained on the phone, I was born with psychic ability—I receive my contacts from the deceased in the form of visions and pulls."

"Pulls?" Alex asked without cynicism in his tone. He had seemed to overcome some of his original skepticism during their phone conversation.

Jenny nodded. "I get led to places of significance. Recently, while I was driving from Tennessee to Georgia, I was led to a house at the end of Beverly Court."

The couple exchanged glances.

"I was invited in to the house by the current owner. There I saw a distinct image of what happened that fateful day back in 1988." Jenny leaned forward onto her elbows. "I am quite sure your son didn't murder Stella Jorgenson."

"I know that," Kim said softly. "I never doubted that for a minute."

Jenny looked at this woman, who had endured both her son's wrongful imprisonment and his early death, and her heart positively ached. "Well, I'm going to try to prove that. Officially."

Alex chimed in. "You do know he passed away years ago, don't you?"

"I do," Jenny said with a nod, "but I also know his soul would be able to rest better if he could be exonerated. I think even now that's important to him."

Kim looked down at her lap.

"Not only that," Jenny added, trying to remain unemotional, "true justice hasn't been served for Stella yet. I'd like to figure out who did this so he can be properly punished. So far, your son has been the only one to pay any kind of price for her murder."

A long moment of silence ensued. Eventually, Alex said, "Well, I do appreciate your efforts."

"Thank you," Jenny replied. She clasped her fingers together and added, "I was wondering if I could count on you to help me in my investigation. Would you be willing to answer some questions about Nate and about that day?"

"Sure," Kim said, "we'll tell you anything you want to know."

Jenny sat on the couch next to Kim, who had brought out old photo albums. "Here's little Nate as a baby."

Jenny was getting more than she'd bargained for. However, when she considered everything this family had been through, she resolved to look at every last photo and listen to every last story. It was the least she could do for these people who had been dealt so much injustice.

She glanced down at the picture being presented to her, noting the stitches that ran vertically up baby Nate's upper lip. "He was born with a cleft lip and palate," Kim explained, "but he was a fighter, and he got through those surgeries like a champ."

Jenny focused on the baby's eyes, which would go on to eventually witness horrors that no one should ever be forced to see. With a smile plastered on her face, she said, "He certainly was a little cutie."

"Yes, he was," Kim said with affectionate reflection. "His brother looked just like him…aside from the cleft, of course." She put her hand on Jenny's arm and added, "I've often said if it wasn't for that little scar, I wouldn't ever know whose baby pictures I was looking at."

"Was his brother older or younger?" Jenny asked.

"Younger. Nate was the oldest of my three boys."

She flipped some more pages in the photo album, eventually reaching images of an older baby in the hospital with an IV in his arm. "Oh," Kim said as if she'd previously forgotten. "This was one of his many trips to the hospital. He was forever fighting infections. He practically lived with a fever." She touched her hand to her chin as she recalled, "But even still, he was always such a happy child. I think he didn't know any different. A little one who is constantly sick doesn't know what it's like to feel well."

Jenny placed her hand on her belly; this was a painful exercise to say the least. However, out of respect, she continued to listen.

Eventually, pictures of a school-aged boy graced the pages. One photo featured him holding an award and wearing a smile as wide as the moon. Jenny pointed to the image. "What was that award for?"

"Citizenship," Kim explained. "School was never his thing, grade-wise. No matter how hard he worked, he always came home with below-average marks." She called to her husband. "What did they say his IQ was? Was it seventy-four?"

"Seventy-two," Alex stated flatly.

Seventy-two. Jenny recalled that in the school where she used to teach, children qualified for services if their IQ was seventy or below. The kids with IQs slightly above that always managed to slip through the cracks.

Those were the cases that always broke Jenny's heart, and this was certainly proving to be no exception.

Kim continued with her story. "But he was a kind child. The teachers always raved about how nice and polite he was, even if he struggled to pay attention to the studies. One of them said Nate would have been willing to buy sand in the desert if he thought saying no would have hurt your feelings." She glanced at the picture and smiled. "But, boy, was he ever delighted to get this award. Do you remember that day, Alex? He was in, what, third grade?"

"Yup. Third grade."

Kim turned to Jenny. "His teacher had called us and told us he was getting an award and we should come to the school for the assembly. It was a surprise, though, so we sat in the back of the auditorium. Fortunately, he didn't notice us there. When they called his name, he practically sprinted to the stage. Do you remember that, Alex?"

"Yup. I remember."

"Oh, what a day that was."

Jenny noticed how much love and happiness exuded from Kim's face. It was almost too much to bear.

At that moment a wave washed over Jenny. Kim continued to talk, but her words became distant, replaced instead by the voices in Jenny's own mind.

She saw a much younger version of Kim sitting across from her on the other side of a glass partition, holding a black phone to her ear. Jenny heard a male voice resonate from within her. "They had pork chops for dinner last night."

Kim smiled lovingly. "You always did love your pork chops."

"With mashed potatoes, too."

"Ah, yes," Kim replied. "It isn't the same without those mashed potatoes."

A short silence ensued, after which Kim added, "Well, baby, my time here is almost up."

Jenny placed her masculine hand flat against the glass, and Kim did the same on her side. "You know I didn't do it, right mama?"

"I know, baby. You don't have it in you."

"'Cause I can be okay in here if you know I didn't do it."

A mixture of pain, love and sadness graced Kim's face. "I know you didn't do it."

"Dad, too?"

"Your dad, too."

Kim's present voice took over as the image dissolved in Jenny's mind. "I'm sorry," Jenny said as she interrupted, "but I just got a message from Nate."

Kim immediately stopped talking and looked at Jenny. "You did?"

"Well, maybe *message* isn't the right word—but I did just get a vision." She smiled and looked at Kim. "I understand Nate liked pork chops and mashed potatoes."

While her face remained expressionless, Kim began to laugh. "Really? That's it? That's the message?" She turned to her husband. "Did you hear that, Alex? Nate communicates from beyond the grave and he talks about pork chops and mashed potatoes."

Alex let out a hearty chuckle. "That sounds about right. That boy always did like his food."

"It sounds like he'd get along quite well with my husband," Jenny said with a smile. "But Nate did clue me in on one other thing..." Her voice became much more serious. "He let me know that he was okay with being in jail, as long as you two knew he was innocent."

Kim sat back in the couch and placed her hands on her lap. The joy left her face as she let out a long breath. "That's what he always said," she admitted. "Our approval was all he ever needed. He said that every time we were about to leave the prison."

Jenny placed her hand on top of Kim's. "Well, I'd like to prove his innocence to the world." Eager to get down to business, Jenny repositioned herself so she could look directly at Kim. "I'd like to talk about what happened that day, if you're willing."

Kim slowly closed the photo album. With a serious expression, she whispered, "I'm willing."

"Why don't you tell me what you know to be true about that day, and I'll see if it matches up with what I've seen."

Kim looked up at Alex for a moment of support; then, she turned her gaze toward Jenny. "Nate was outside, doing yard work. He was pulling weeds from the flower bed out front. That's when he said he heard some screams coming from next door. He went over to check it out, and he said the front door was open...the wood door, anyway. The screen door was closed.

"He said he called in from the front stoop, saying 'Miss Stella? Miss Megan? Are you two alright?'" Kim looked down at her lap. "Remember what I said about Nate being polite? He would have never gone into the house without being invited in...even if there were screams."

Jenny wondered if Nate had been a little less concerned with manners—or even just a tiny bit smarter—if he could have caught a glimpse of the person who really did this.

Kim continued, "He said he heard a yell for help, so at that point he opened the door and went inside. He said he saw Stella lying there, bleeding. He went over to help her and got bloody in the process. He even picked up the knife because he was curious about it. He brought that knife home with him when he came back to call 9-1-1."

"So, that's why he ran back home? To call the police?" Jenny asked.

"That was his intent, but he never made the call," Kim confessed.

"He didn't? Why not?"

Kim let out a sigh that indicated she wished she had the ability to rewrite history. "You're probably too young to remember this, but back in the eighties, there were no cell phones. There were only home phones. We had three teenagers in the house, so we had phones in just about every room. It was only one phone line, mind you, but we had five or six phones. The problem with that is if one of the phones doesn't get hung up properly, you can't make an outgoing call. It's like all of the phones are off the hook. So, Nate tried to call the police, but he wasn't able to. He couldn't figure out which phone was the problem."

Jenny squinted and rubbed her temples. "If he had been able to make the call, things may have been different for him."

Kim seemed solemn. "I believe they would have been. Not only that, but the man across the street saw Nate running from the house with blood-stained clothes and the knife in his hand. Couple that with the fact that he never called the police—and that he had scratches all over his arms from the weeding—and that he *confessed* for some outlandish reason...Even I have to admit that boy looked guilty as sin."

Jenny had to agree. Had she not had divine insight, she would have probably believed in his guilt as well.

"Well, this has been some very helpful information," Jenny said. "It matches up with all of the visions I have had. Hopefully, I'll be able to convince the authorities that this is what really happened, and Nate's name will be cleared."

"That would be nice," Kim said. She then looked at her lap and added, "Although, I'm not sure how much good that would do."

Jenny smiled. "It would do a lot of good...for his soul, anyway."

Kim managed half a smile.

"But Mr. and Mrs. Minnick, can I ask you something?"

"Sure, honey," Kim replied. "What is it?"

"Do you know of anyone who might have done this? Someone who may have had something against Stella?"

Both of Nate's parents shook their heads. "We barely knew her," Alex said. "She could have had all the enemies in the world and we wouldn't have known anything about it."

Feeling as though the couple had been through enough for one day, Jenny staged her exit, promising to be in touch if she came up with any answers. The Minnicks vowed to do the same.

As soon as Jenny got in her car, she dialed Kyle. After explaining what she had learned from Nate's parents, she asked if he had been able to uncover any new details in the case.

"Well, I've determined that there was never a real investigation of the crime," he began. "Nate Minnick was the only suspect ever named. Because of that, we're looking at ground zero in terms of investigation. I've put in a call to Megan Patterson, formerly Megan Casey, who used to be Stella's roommate. I imagine if Stella had an enemy running around out there, Megan would be the most likely person to know about it."

"You're probably right," Jenny agreed. After a moment of thought she added, "You do realize I'm going to be of minimal help to you. Ordinarily, I can gain insight from the victim, leading me in the direction of who did it, but in this case Nate doesn't know who the perpetrator was. He's just letting me know it wasn't him."

"Stella won't be able to tell you?"

Jenny remained quiet for a little while; Kyle had touched on a very important point. Why hadn't Stella herself contacted Jenny? If she had been taken so brutally, why didn't she want her story told? Had she crossed, despite the nature of her demise?

"I can't say for sure, but I think the answer to that question is *no*." She contemplated one more minute before adding. "Although, I really would like to know why that's the case."

Chapter 6

"That was painful," Jenny said as she slid under the covers, referring to the evening with Zack and Andy. "Watching you two go at it is like watching two kids bicker at recess."

"See? This is why I didn't bring you around him before this. I didn't want you to be exposed to it."

"Is it that you didn't want me to be exposed to it, or you didn't want me to see it until after we were married and I was committed?"

"Why?" he said with a laugh. "Would you have backed out of the wedding if you saw it ahead of time?"

"I would have had more thinking to do, that's for sure." Jenny cuddled up next to him and added, "Seriously, you two need to cut each other some slack."

"Well, you saw him. No matter what you say to him, he turns it into something negative. It's impossible to have a decent conversation with the man."

Jenny leaned up on one elbow. "Okay, I'm going play devil's advocate for a minute here."

"Uh-oh."

"Don't be scared," she said. "I just want you to think about this from your father's point of view. I mean, I know last night he was harping on you about not being responsible enough—or financially ready—to have a baby. But you have to consider what sparked the argument that has kept you from speaking for the last few months—you stopped showing up at your job. *With his company.* You didn't call; you didn't officially quit. He had to call you to find out where you had been, and that's when you told him you weren't going to be working for him anymore. To be fair, I think anyone would be mad about that." She winced as she added, "And it does kind of make you look irresponsible."

"Yeah, but the only reason I did that was because he was an asshole of a boss."

"I understand." Jenny gently brushed a stray hair off of Zack's forehead. "But he doesn't see it that way."

Zack didn't respond.

"And," she remarked as she tapped him on the chest, "it appears to me that you purposely avoid mentioning things that would make him proud of you." She reduced her tone to reflect her compassion. "Why didn't you tell him about your plan to renovate Rob's house?"

"Because he'd want to help me."

"Is that so bad?"

"You've seen the two of us together. Yes, it's bad."

"It might be a nice olive branch."

"Maybe." Zack shrugged with one shoulder. "But somehow I doubt it."

Jenny could see she wasn't going to get anywhere with this conversation, so she switched gears. "Well, I have a little research project I'd like to embark on." She rolled over off of Zack's shoulder and reached for her laptop on her end table.

"What's that?"

"Well," she said as opened the computer and propped up against the headboard. "I'm just a little bit too troubled by the conversation I had with the Minnicks today. I found out that Nate was born with a cleft lip and palate, he battled chronic illness as a child, he had a very low IQ *and* a congenital heart defect—and that's just not sitting right with me."

"Do you think they were making it all up?"

"Oh, I'm positive they weren't; that isn't the problem." She turned away from the computer and looked at Zack. "Have you ever taken a probability course?"

"Is that a serious question?"

Jenny stifled a laugh. "I'll take that as a *no*." She typed a few buttons and briefly skimmed the information that popped up. "See, it says here that roughly one in a thousand babies are born with cleft lips and palates."

"That is pretty rare."

After a few more keystrokes, she said, "And about three percent of people have IQs in the mentally retarded range..."

"I don't get it," Zack said. "Are you worried about our baby?"

She shook her head. "No." Jenny thought about it for a second and acknowledged, "Well, yes, but that's not what's motivating me at the moment." She turned to Zack. "In my probability class, I leaned that if two events are unrelated, you need to multiply their probabilities together if you want to find the likelihood of both things happening."

He looked at her expressionlessly for a long time before simply saying, "Huh?"

Jenny laughed. "If there's a three percent chance that a baby will be born retarded and a point-one percent chance a baby will be born with a cleft, then the probability that a baby would be born with both conditions would be point-zero-zero-three percent. That's three babies out of one-hundred-thousand."

"Wow," Zack said, "I guess poor Nate was pretty unlucky."

"If you throw in the chronic infections and the heart defect, then the odds of one child having all of that would be even slimmer." Jenny held up her finger. "*But,* you'll notice I said that's only true if the conditions are *unrelated*. I just can't help but think something bigger is going on here; it's too unlikely that this one baby would have those four separate, relatively rare issues." She made a face that reflected her sympathy. "If I had to guess, I would say Nate had only one condition that manifested itself in four different ways."

"Well done, Sherlock." Zack patted Jenny's leg. "What do you think he had?"

"That, I don't know...but I'd like to find out."

Zack was quiet for a moment before he posed, "Don't you think his doctors would have considered this?"

Jenny shrugged. "Maybe. Probably. But it can't hurt to investigate, right?"

Time ticked by as she scoured multiple websites; Zack's breathing became heavy next to her, and she also found herself eager to sleep, but first she wanted an answer. After what seemed like an eternity, she read an article that finally seemed to have everything she was looking for. With a smile she leaned back into her pillows, pointing at her computer screen.

"Bingo."

"It's called Chromosome Twenty-Two Deletion," Jenny announced at the breakfast table, "and all of Nate's symptoms can be attributed to it."

"Really?" Ellen asked. "I wonder why the doctors didn't recognize that earlier."

"Well, it wasn't discovered until the early nineties, which is when he passed away." She held up her hand. "Actually, that's not entirely true. Doctors had noticed that those conditions often went hand-in-hand in the seventies and eighties, but they didn't know what caused it until later...too late for Nate to ever be diagnosed."

"What does cause it?" Zack asked.

"It's a chromosomal disorder," Jenny said. "A little piece of the twenty-second chromosome is missing."

"All of that happens because one piece of one chromosome is missing? Dear Lord," Zack said. "If it's that easy to get jacked up, it's a miracle any of us are born normal."

Jenny stuck her fingers in her ears and sang, "La la la la. I can't hear you."

"Sorry," he said, holding up his hand. "Not something I should say in front of a pregnant woman."

"Especially since it's not always hereditary," Jenny said. "In a lot of cases, it's just something that goes wrong during pregnancy. It could happen to any of us."

"Okay," Ellen remarked with a look of concern, "I don't want to think about that. So...it's great that you found this out, but do you think it will do anything to help your case?"

"Maybe," Jenny replied. "I want to argue that Nate's confession was not reliable. If I can say that he suffered from a chromosomal disorder, perhaps the appropriate people will be willing to find some kind of legal snag that would make his confession inadmissible."

Ellen frowned as she considered the approach. "Sounds reasonable enough, although I have to admit I don't know anything about the law."

"Unfortunately, I don't either," Jenny confessed. "This is all just speculation at this point." The buzz of her phone interrupted her statement; she glanced at the caller. "It's Kyle Buchanan," she announced. "I wonder what he wants so early in the morning." She excused herself to answer the call. "Well, hello, world's best private investigator."

"Good morning to you, my psychic friend."

Jenny laughed. "To what do I owe the honor?"

"Well, I was able to track down Megan Patterson, Stella's roommate."

"Ooh," Jenny replied with excitement. She flashed a sideways smile at Zack and Ellen. "I guess now I know what I'm going to be doing today."

The years had been kind to Megan; her face was relatively free of wrinkles, and her shoulder-length auburn hair looked like it was still her natural color. She sat on the couch, listening to Jenny's story, looking like she was making a concerted effort to avoid tears. Jenny sat on a leather chair across from her, notepad in hand. "I'm trying to accomplish two things," she said in conclusion. "I want to prove that Nate Minnick didn't actually kill Stella that day, and I'd like to find out who did."

Looking white as a sheet, Megan cleared her throat and weakly said, "Wow. I have to admit, this is quite unexpected. I've spent the last twenty-six years believing the right person was behind bars."

"Sadly, I don't think that's true," Jenny proclaimed.

With her hands shaking, Megan released a slow, anxiety-filled breath. "I hate to think the person who did this has been out on the streets all this time." She raised her eyes to meet Jenny's. "I still have nightmares, you know. What happened to Stella—it terrifies me to this day."

"I can imagine," Jenny said compassionately. "I am under the impression you weren't home when the attack happened?"

She shook her head. "No, I was at the movies. I've often thought that it could have just as easily been me...I could have been killed alongside her or even instead of her, if only I had been home."

"You think it was more random as opposed to Stella being the intended target?"

"I don't know what to think anymore," Megan said disconcertedly. "All this time I have been operating under the assumption that Nate had just snapped one day. I didn't think he had anything specific against Stella, so I always believed I would have been a perfectly acceptable victim had my plans been different that day."

"Tell me," Jenny said as she leaned forward on her elbows, "were you truly comfortable that they had the right person? Did you honestly believe Nate had something like that in him?"

Megan seemed to give the question some thought. "I do have to admit I was surprised when it turned out to be him—he'd always seemed like a nice kid. I know he was a little slow, but he appeared to be harmless enough. The evidence against him was just so overwhelming that I did believe the jury got it right." She let out a nervous laugh. "That didn't stop the nightmares, though."

Jenny closed her eyes for a moment; murder never only had one victim. Sticking to the matter at hand, she posed, "If you remove Nate from the equation, is there anyone you can think of who might have wanted Stella dead?"

Jenny could tell right away that she had struck a nerve; Megan's expression left no question about that. With a whisper she said, "I can think of a couple."

A couple. This was more than Jenny had bargained for. "Why don't you tell me a little bit about those people?"

Megan looked troubled.

"I won't judge," Jenny assured her, "if that's what you're worried about."

After several moments of wringing her hands, Megan began her story. "First, I want to let you know that Stella was once happily married. She had the life that most of us only dreamed about—great husband, successful career, nice house."

This was news to Jenny. "What happened?"

She drew in a breath. "Her husband was killed in a car accident."

Jenny jotted the notes down on her pad. "When did that happen?"

"About two years before she was killed, I guess?"

"What became of Stella after that?"

"Well, she kept her job as a nurse at Saint Mary's hospital, but she had to sell her house. She couldn't afford to keep it on her own, which is why she and I rented a place together."

"I assume you two worked together?"

"We were co-workers, yes...and friends. We had been working together at the hospital for a couple of years at that point." Megan looked at her lap. "For a while after the accident, Stella became a complete recluse. She would go to work and back, run just the essential errands, but other than that she never left the house. She never left her *bed.* She stayed in a state of depression like that for months."

"About how many months?"

Megan scratched her head. "Four? Six? Something like that. It was a long time, and it was very painful to watch. I kept encouraging her to go out from time to time—nothing involving men, mind you, but just a nice dinner with friends or something." She shook her head. "No matter how hard I tried, she just wouldn't go."

"I assume that changed."

"Yes, it did. On her anniversary," Megan said softly. "Or I guess I should say, what would have been her anniversary. She had that night off from work, but I didn't. When I came home in the evening, she was just about as drunk as she could be, and she told me she wanted to go out."

"Did you?"

"Yes, we went to a dance club." She looked as if she felt horribly guilty. "She brought a guy home with her that night."

Jenny remained silent.

"I tried to convince her not to, but she was determined. She just kept saying that the night was too unbearable, and she couldn't spend it alone. She needed to feel arms around her. I knew she wished they were Pete's arms, but she was willing to settle for second best."

"Did she develop a relationship with this man that she brought home?"

Megan shook her head. "She never saw him again." She looked as if she was ratting out her best friend.

"Remember, I'm not here to judge," Jenny said with a compassionate smile. "I'm only here to find out who did this to her."

A small tear worked its way down Megan's cheek as she nodded with understanding.

"Was that man one of the people you believe was capable of killing her?"

"No," she replied confidently. "There were many more like him. Too many to count, actually. She went on a bit of a…spree."

Jenny found her heart aching for Stella, who clearly hadn't wanted to live like that. She surely wanted to grow old with the man she had married, but that wasn't her fate. Jenny could only imagine every stranger she brought home was a desperate attempt at recapturing what she had felt for only one person—a man that had been taken from her too soon. In addition, the world probably didn't understand her actions; plenty of unfavorable names must have been thrown her way by people who, mercifully, never had to walk in her shoes.

Life was horribly unfair sometimes.

Remaining professional, Jenny asked, "So did *any* of those men make the suspect list?"

Megan nodded. "Toward the end, yes. She started to get *involved* with some of them—and by that I mean she had some casual relationships. At the time she was killed, she was seeing two different men. Those were the guys I was thinking of."

"Can you tell me a little about those guys?"

Becoming less emotional, Megan said, "Well, one of them was Doctor Burke."

"Doctor Burke?" Jenny wrote as she spoke. "What was his first name?"

"Shane."

"Was he someone you worked with at the hospital?"

"He was. He was quite a bit older than Stella…and married."

While Jenny didn't outwardly react, bells went off inside her head.

"Did the wife know about the affair?"

"I don't think so," Megan said. "She had a successful career of her own and traveled a lot. As far as I know, she was oblivious to what was happening back at home."

"Did you know Doctor Burke well?"

"I did." Megan sighed as she recalled the details. "I worked many of the same shifts that he did, and I also saw him outside of work when he started seeing Stella."

"What was your opinion of him?"

"I wasn't crazy about him. I mean, he was nice and all, but how upstanding could his character have been if he was cheating on his wife every time she went out of town?"

Jenny looked up at Megan with just her eyes. "Do you think he was capable of murder?"

"I never thought so," Megan confessed. "But who knows? If Nate didn't do this, clearly somebody did."

"Do you think his feelings for Stella were genuine?"

"Do I think his feelings were genuine?" she repeated as she contemplated. Eventually she settled on an explanation. "I think his ego was genuinely inflated by her interest in him. She was fifteen years younger than him and very attractive, and for that reason she was valuable to him."

"So, he didn't really care about her?"

"He cared that she helped him look good."

Jenny's pen scribbled down notes. "What do you think would have happened if she tried to break up with him?"

"Oh, I don't have to guess about that—it actually happened a few times. As soon as it looked like Stella was about to pull away, suddenly there would be flowers and jewelry and romantic weekend getaways." Megan covered her face with her hands and muttered, "My God, I'm making Stella out to sound so bad." She lowered her hands and added, "I assure you, she wasn't a gold-digger. It wasn't about the material possessions for her at all. It was about that feeling of magic. It was about someone paying attention to her." She looked heartbroken. "It was about trying to regain what she'd lost."

"I'd gathered that," Jenny said reassuringly.

Megan nodded in acknowledgement. "Even though I understood why it was happening, it was still difficult to watch. I hated knowing that she was part of an affair. She was better than that, but I was afraid to ever say anything to her about it. I mean, I had a boyfriend at the time—that I later went on to marry—and he was very much alive. I didn't feel like I could criticize her lifestyle having never lost a man I loved so tragically. Who knows? Maybe I would have done the same thing if I had ended up in her situation." She shrugged and looked down.

Jenny was finding *this* to be painful to watch. "Well, the reason I'm asking about all of this is because an affair might be a motive for murder. Is it possible that Stella may have threatened to go to Mrs. Burke and tell her about the relationship?"

Megan shook her head. "I sincerely doubt it. Stella was not a vindictive person. She was needy, yes, but not evil. To be quite honest, I don't think she cared enough about Doctor Burke to try to break up his marriage. That would have implied that she wanted him for herself, and that wasn't the case." She raised her eyes to meet Jenny's. "Stella wouldn't have had multiple lovers if she'd had genuine feelings for any of them."

A valid point indeed. "Well, that leaves Mrs. Burke. Had you ever met her?"

Megan nodded. "Yes, a few times. At work functions."

The implications were not lost on Jenny. "Was Stella at these work functions?"

"She was."

"Oh, dear," Jenny remarked. "How did that go?"

"Surprisingly well," Megan said. "It was actually a bit unnerving to see how easily Stella could smile and make small talk with the Burkes at the Christmas party considering she'd been sleeping with Doctor Burke for the weeks leading up to it."

For a brief moment, Jenny sympathized greatly with Mrs. Doctor Burke. There was so much wrong with that scenario.

"Do you think Mrs. Burke had any idea this affair was going on?"

"Well, she didn't seem concerned or upset at all around Stella, so I assume she didn't know."

"You said she was a successful businesswoman, though, which would imply she was very smart. Do you really think it's possible she didn't know about the affairs?"

Megan responded only by raising her eyebrows and shrugging.

After quietly deliberating the situation for a moment, Jenny switched gears. "Okay, you said Stella had been seeing two men when she was killed. Who was the other?"

"A guy named Colin Barrymore. He lived in an apartment complex behind the house. They'd met at a club a few months earlier, and they had been dating casually ever since."

"What was he like?"

"Young," Megan said emphatically. "Very young. I think he was twenty-one, maybe? He was still in school...he went to Braynard College full time." Once again Megan looked sad. "Unlike Doctor Burke, I think this poor kid was very much in love with Stella. You know, the whole *successful older woman* thing."

"Did he think he was the only one she was dating?"

"I can't say for sure...well, actually I can." A troubled expression crossed Megan's face. "Oh, dear."

"What's the matter?"

"I'm just remembering that cookout," Megan said, mostly to herself, as she was clearly immersed in thought.

Jenny allowed her to fully recollect the memory.

With a deep breath, Megan explained. "The weekend before Stella was killed, we had a small cookout at the house, and somehow Doctor Burke and Colin both showed up. She was usually much too careful to allow that to happen, but this time she must have gotten her signals crossed."

"What happened?"

"I'm trying to remember," Megan whispered, looking distant. "The barbeque started in the late afternoon, I think, and Doctor Burke was there as Stella's date." She covered her face with her hands. "They'd even snuck off to her bedroom when he'd first gotten there. Oh, God." She looked up again and shooed the idea away with her hand. "Anyway, the afternoon seemed perfectly normal until shortly after dinner—when Colin arrived."

Jenny took furious notes as Megan told the story.

"Stella and Doctor Burke were sitting cuddled up together on the couch when Colin walked in. He had flowers for Stella. Imagine the poor kid's surprise when he walked in to find another man with his arm around the woman he thought was his girlfriend."

"Was there a fight?" Jenny asked with wide eyes.

"Almost. Colin was angry, demanding to know who Doctor Burke was. Doctor Burke stood up and asked the same thing of Colin. It looked like things could have gotten out of hand, but Stella took charge of the situation."

"How did she do that?"

Megan sighed as she recalled the scene. "She asked Colin to step outside with her. I'm not sure what she said to him, but he ended up leaving. When she came back inside, I heard her tell Doctor Burke that Colin was just some young neighborhood kid who had a crush on her and showed up from time to time. Doctor Burke asked if she needed him to take care of it for her, and she declined. She said she'd be fine. For the next hour or so, everything went back to normal.

"Doctor Burke had to leave early," Megan continued. "I think he had a surgery the next morning, or his wife was coming home, or something like that. Either way, he left before the sun went down." She let out a little sound of disgust and shook her head. "And wouldn't you know it—with one phone call, there was Colin, back at the house. He took over right where Doctor Burke had left off." She leaned back in her seat and folded her arms. "He even spent the night."

Jenny was surprised. "He was willing to come back after she'd sent him away?"

"Strangely enough, he was. Stella had managed to convince him that her apparent interest in Doctor Burke was strictly a necessary evil in trying to advance her career. She thanked Colin for being willing to hide out that extra hour so he wouldn't *blow her cover*." She made finger quotes. "You know, I've got to give Stella credit. I realize a lot of folks wouldn't have approved of what she was doing, but she did have this way about her that allowed her to get away with things that most people wouldn't even dream of trying. She probably said something to Doctor Burke like, *why would I want a kid when I could have a real, mature man like you?* Only to turn around and tell Colin, *what would I want with an old man when I could have a strapping young thing like you?*" Megan once again shook her head. "She had a way with words, that's for sure."

Jenny paused to consider that her *way with words* may have cost Stella her life.

After taking a moment to review her notes, Jenny sat back in her chair and said, "Well, it looks like we may have two viable suspects here—three if you count Mrs. Burke. Now, do you know if these guys were ever questioned by the police?"

Megan gave it some thought, but ultimately answered, "You know, I don't believe they were. The focus was always on Nate Minnick, from the very beginning. I don't think the police really looked into any other scenarios."

"Well," Jenny raised her eyes to meet Megan's, "I think that needs to change."

Chapter 7

"So, how's the land of misfit contractors?" Jenny asked through the phone. She used the speaker function so she could keep both hands on the wheel.

"Kick ass," Zack said proudly. "The carpet in the bedrooms is up, and we've cut into the walls to make the door openings wider. We're still waiting on the county before we start the ramp in the front, but we have plenty to keep us busy in the meantime. Speaking of busy…how's the detective work?"

"I found out some interesting little tidbits," she confessed. "It seems Stella was involved in a little love triangle. She had two boyfriends, and one of them was married."

"Wouldn't that be a love rectangle?"

"Indeed. And love rectangles often don't end well. I've got Kyle looking into the whereabouts of the two guys she was dating, and in the meantime, I'm going to the police station to let them know about my suspicions."

"Do you think they'll re-open the case?"

Jenny shook her head. "I don't know. I have no idea what to expect, really."

"Well, good luck to you," Zack said. "I'm sorry I can't be there."

"Don't worry," Jenny replied with a smile. "You are exactly where you should be right now."

Even though she had never been there before, Jenny felt a wave of familiarity as she approached the police station. She could tell Nate was with her, a notion that still spooked her after all this time. Her eyes searched the area around her, seeing nothing but bright blue skies and a parking lot full of cars. To the naked eye, she seemed alone and everything was normal, but she knew better.

Although Nate was invisible to her, his presence gave her the strength to walk through the door of the station with confidence. She approached the front desk, where a young woman was surrounded by mounds of papers. "Hello," Jenny said professionally, "I was wondering if I could speak to somebody about some information I have on a case."

Jenny was told to have a seat and wait to be called; however, she was feeling a pull that she wanted to pursue. She stared at the double doors that led into the back of the station; she wanted to be on the other side of those doors. This was the first time she was being led to an area where she couldn't go, and she found resisting the tug to be difficult. An uneasiness rose from within her.

Mercifully, it wasn't long before an officer came out into the lobby with an extended hand. "Hi," he said with a pleasant smile, "I'm Detective Dante Wilks."

Jenny shook his hand and replied, "Hi. Jenny Wa—Jenny Larrabee." She flashed an embarrassed smile, knowing how stupid she must have sounded. "I just got married," she explained. "I'm still getting used to it."

"Well, congratulations, Mrs. Larrabee. Why don't you come back with me and tell me what you have for us?"

She followed Detective Wilks into his office, which had glass walls with open blinds. Considering most of the other officers had cubicles in one large room, Jenny determined Detective Wilks must have held a relatively high rank.

He gestured for her to sit down across from him; he did the same in his reclining office chair. Jenny quickly noticed the pictures of the smiling children that graced his desk, and for a fleeting moment she wondered if those kids knew that their father risked his life every time he left for work.

Shooing the thought from her head, Jenny smiled pleasantly as the detective asked for the reason behind her visit.

It was only then that Jenny realized she had nothing rehearsed. "I've been looking into the Stella Jorgenson case," she began, figuring that was as good of a place to start as any. "It was a murder that happened back in 1988. Are you familiar with it?"

"I've heard of it," he replied. "We don't have many cases like that around here, so the few that we do have get remembered."

Jenny smirked. "I guess that's a good thing."

Detective Wilks smiled in return. "I'll be happy if we never have one like that again."

"I can imagine." Jenny felt uncomfortable, knowing she was about to accuse the department of fingering the wrong man. That feeling of uneasiness was compounded by Nate's continued pull, which made her want to leave the office and head back out into the main room with the cubicles. Nonetheless, she continued. "I've come to believe that Nate Minnick may have suffered from a chromosomal disorder which may have compromised his ability to make a reliable confession."

Wilks folded his hands into a steeple in front of his mouth. "You don't think Minnick did it?"

She looked at him unwaveringly. "I'm quite sure he didn't."

"Well, then, who do you think it was?"

With much less confidence, Jenny replied. "I don't know yet. I'm looking into a few possibilities right now—Stella was dating two men at the time of her murder, and one of them was married."

Wilks shook his head. "If you don't know who did it, what makes you so sure it wasn't Minnick?"

A mental debate ensued inside Jenny's head. Ultimately, she decided that actions would speak louder than words. "I know this is unorthodox, but would you be willing to follow me for a minute?"

"Follow you? To where?"

"Not outside the building," Jenny replied. That was the best she could answer considering she also didn't know where they'd be going.

Wilks looked at her strangely for a moment before gesturing his hand toward his office door.

Jenny felt an immediate sense of relief as she allowed herself to follow the pull that had been growing inside of her. She led Wilks out of his office and through the maze of cubicles that littered the main room, ultimately bringing him to the opposite wall. She found herself looking at a collage of framed photographs, featuring decorated officers from generations past. One of the pictures in particular caught her eye. She looked at the face as it stared back at her; the man's eyes seemed to come alive from behind the glass. Jenny felt afraid of the man—shamed by him—so she knew she was looking at the right face. "It's him," Jenny said as she pointed to his portrait. "This is the man who conducted Nate Minnick's interrogation."

Before Detective Wilks had the chance to reply, Jenny added, "There's more." The pull continued to lead her, this time around the edge of the room to a door that was closed. She was encouraged that the detective still followed her—she realized she must have looked like a crazy woman. "Is there any way we can get on the other side of this door?" she asked with her gaze fixed firmly on the knob.

Since the ensuing silence was long, she turned to look at Wilks, who appeared to be debating the question. "I guess we can go back here, sure. What the hell?" He opened the door and gestured that she go though.

Immediately, she was drawn down the hall to the second door on the left. It stood slightly ajar with a dark room lurking behind the slim opening. Jenny slowly opened the door and took a couple of steps into the black room. She was aware that Wilks had turned on the light, although she had already closed her eyes and covered her face with her hands by the time he had done so. Standing motionlessly, she absorbed the message Nate intended her to receive, which in this instance came in the form of still shots, like a series of photographs with no sound.

Once the message subsided, Jenny knew her first task was to ensure she appeared to be a credible psychic as opposed to a raving lunatic; she decided the best way to achieve that was to describe the factors that would let Wilks know she'd had a legitimate vision. "The officer," she said, pointing back out toward the main room. "The officer who conducted the interrogation...he smoked. He leaned forward on the desk, getting in Nate's face a lot, pointing at him with two fingers that had a cigarette in between. He wore a really big ring, and he styled his hair in a comb over." She thought a little more before adding, "His clothes didn't match; he wore a diagonally striped tie and a plaid shirt. If you watch the video of the interrogation, I guarantee that's what you will find."

Detective Wilks scratched his short hair and squinted. "So, what you're telling me is that you've just...*seen*...Nate's confession."

Jenny did her best to appear sane. "I have an ability that most people don't have," she said softly. "If you do a little research on me, you'll find that I'm legitimate. In fact, I worked with Bill Abernathy from the Evansdale police department not too long ago. You can ask him about me, if you'd like."

"I know Bill; we go way back." Wilks smiled broadly and shook his head, laughing pleasantly. "I've got to say, this is a first for me."

"It usually is," Jenny replied. "I'm going to be honest," she continued, "I don't even know for sure what I'm trying to accomplish by coming here today. I don't know if I want you to re-open the case, or let me look at some evidence so I can pursue it myself, or if I just wanted to make you aware that I was looking into it. All I know is that Nate Minnick is desperately trying to prove his innocence..." She glanced at Wilks. "I think mostly for his parents' sake. He wants to show them he didn't do it."

Wilks didn't reply.

"I've met with Nate's parents," she added, remembering the photographs of the children on Wilks' desk. "They seem like very nice people. My heart really goes out to them." She looked at the detective out of the corner of her eye. "Nate was born with a lot of issues. He had a cleft lip and palate at birth, was hospitalized a lot throughout his childhood with chronic infections, and his IQ was very low. As a parent, I'm sure you can imagine how tough that was for the Minnicks."

The detective simply grunted in response, looking uncomfortable.

"Then Nate got accused of this murder, and he certainly would have been no match for a trained interrogator. Nate's IQ was seventy-two—he functioned at the level of a child. Of course he signed the confession that was presented to him; that's what he was told to do. And then," Jenny added, realizing this last blow was the cruelest twist of them all, "Nate died in prison at age twenty-one from a congenital heart defect. Can you imagine what that was like for his parents?"

With that, Detective Wilks winced and shook his head; Jenny knew she had struck a nerve.

"I saw you have two children," Jenny said softly.

"I do," he replied in an equally hushed tone. "Jasmine and Demitrius."

"They look beautiful and healthy," Jenny noted, placing her hand on her pregnant belly. "I'm expecting my first child in November, and healthy is all I can hope for. I can't even imagine what the Minnicks went through, having a child with all those difficulties, and the blows just kept on coming for them." She shook her head. "I think that's part of the reason I'm so determined to bring them some answers. I'd like to be able to deliver them some good news for once. They've endured so much." She looked intently at the detective. "All they wanted was a child…just like you and I did. Only they weren't so lucky."

Wilks wiped his hand over the top of his head. "Okay, I can pull up his file and look for some inconsistencies, but I have to warn you that I'm very busy. I don't know how much time I'm going to have to pursue a case that's been closed for two and a half decades."

Jenny smiled with relief. "I can do the digging…all I need is the material to dig through."

He nodded and gestured to the door. As Jenny proceeded to walk out, he turned the lights off behind them. "I'll see what I can get for you, okay? And by the way…"

She looked at him as they headed toward his office.

"That chain-smoking detective you described? That was Sergeant Finneran. He was here when I first started." He smiled and added, "And he never wore matching clothes."

The house was large, as would be expected when its occupant had spent a lifetime being a doctor. The circular driveway in front housed a Lexus and a Jaguar; Jenny concluded that some other expensive cars may have been hidden behind the closed garage doors.

She turned to Kyle as they headed up the front stoop. "Do you want to do the talking or should I?"

"I can," he replied. "When I show people the private investigator identification, it usually scares the hell out of them. That might be a good way to start...catch him off guard and frighten him a little."

She nodded as she pressed the doorbell. A gray-haired, well-put-together woman answered the call. Jenny assumed she was looking at Mrs. Doctor Burke, and she wasn't sure if this woman had been a simple victim of infidelity or the perpetrator of a brutal murder. By the looks of her that day, she hardly seemed the murdering type. "Can I help you?" she asked pleasantly.

"Katherine Burke?" Kyle began, flashing his identification.

A look of worry immediately graced her face. "Yes?"

"My name is Kyle Buchanan; I'm a private investigator looking into the murder of a Ms. Stella Jorgenson back in 1988. I believe she was affiliated with your husband through the hospital where he worked, and I'd like to ask him a few questions if he's available."

She furrowed her brow and placed her hand on her chin. "Yes, I know of her, but I thought that case was solved years ago."

"It was closed, yes," Kyle agreed, "but after all this time we're not sure if the right person was convicted."

"Oh, dear," Mrs. Burke said, looking worried. She turned back into the house and called for her husband, who appeared quickly in the doorway.

"Shane Burke?" Kyle asked.

"Yes."

"I was wondering if I could ask you a few questions about Stella Jorgenson's murder."

Jenny watched with awe as Shane turned to his wife and easily convinced her that he wanted to have the discussion elsewhere—to protect her from unpleasant details of the murder. The descriptions may have been gruesome, he explained, and those weren't images he wanted his wife to have to live with going forward.

Charming, Jenny thought. *He was then, and he is now.* Although, she gathered *deceitful* and *manipulative* could have just as easily been used to describe him, both then and now.

Doctor Burke walked with Jenny and Kyle out to a screened-in gazebo, complete with three ceiling fans that provided a delightful breeze. They sat at a glass-top table with chairs that boasted thick, comfortable cushions. Jenny found herself jealous of this little hideaway; it would have been a great place to spend an afternoon reading. She wondered if that was a luxury the Burkes deserved to have considering what one or both of them might have done all those years ago.

"So, I assume you remember Stella Jorgenson?" Kyle began.

"Yeah, I remember her."

"I imagine you can recall how she met her demise."

"I can," he said with a nod. "She was stabbed by her neighbor."

"Well, we're not convinced it was her neighbor anymore."

Jenny watched as Shane's expression changed into a look she couldn't immediately recognize. Was she observing fear? Concern? Shock? She felt helpless that she didn't have the aid of spirits guiding her in the right direction this time. Like all of the detectives she'd ever worked with in the past, this time she was forced to rely solely on testimony, body language, evidence and intuition.

She liked it better when the spirits showed her the face of the killer.

"I understand that you and Stella were involved in a romantic relationship at the time the murder took place," Kyle said calmly.

"Just prior to it, yes."

Just prior to it?

"The relationship ended before she was killed?" Kyle posed. "Is that what you're telling me?"

"Yes, that's what I'm telling you."

This was all news to Jenny. She was hoping the look on her face didn't give away her surprise.

"Doctor Burke, we have eyewitness testimony saying you spent the weekend prior to the murder at a cookout at Stella's house."

He nodded. "That is true."

"So, your relationship ended during the last week of her life?" Kyle asked.

"It did. In fact, it ended because there was some crazy kid in her neighborhood who was obsessed with her. If you want to find your murderer, you should look for that guy. I bet he had something to do with it."

Jenny interjected, "Colin Barrymore."

"I guess that was his name," Shane said with a dismissive gesture of his hand. "I don't even know."

Kyle continued the line of questioning. "How did he cause the break-up of your relationship?"

"Well, he had shown up the weekend before at Stella's house when I was there. He was bringing her flowers. He saw us together, and we were clearly *together*. I guess it was too much for him; he made a terrible scene."

"Doctor Burke," Jenny said professionally, "I've spoken to another person who was there that day; from what I understand, Colin left peacefully after he saw you with Stella. The witness specifically said there was no scene."

"There wasn't a scene at the cookout," the doctor clarified. "When he showed up at the hospital a few days later, that was a different story."

Jenny's eyes widened, but Kyle was the one to respond. "What happened when he came to the hospital?"

"He was like a lunatic," Shane said. "I worked in the ER at the time, and he came wandering in one day looking for me."

Jenny was surprised by what she was hearing. "He was allowed to just wander in?"

"This was the eighties," Doctor Burke explained. "Things were a lot different then. Security was practically non-existent. Anyway, he walked around until he found me...I was setting a kid's broken arm when he started accusing me of forcing Stella to sleep with me so she could keep her job...he said that right in front of this kid and his mother. I told him to get the hell out of my ER, but he persisted. He told me that if I didn't leave Stella alone he'd go to my supervisors and have me fired." He shook his head. "That's when things got to be too much for me. I mean, I liked Stella

71

and all, and I enjoyed spending time with her, but that was crazy. After that incident, I told Stella it might be best if we took a break."

Kyle wrote down notes as he spoke. "And how did she take that news?"

With a shrug, Shane said, "I'm sure she was devastated."

Jenny knew that when she'd look back at this conversation with Doctor Burke later, she was going to find a lot wrong with it. She was going to find a lot wrong with *him*. At the moment, however, she could only sit and listen, trying to make sense of the latest developments.

"Okay, so you two broke up a few days before the murder," Kyle said calmly. "Where were you the afternoon the murder took place?"

"At the hospital," Shane said confidently. "Working."

"Can anyone substantiate that claim?"

"I'm sure somebody can, although I don't know how long the hospital keeps records of that kind of thing."

"This was twenty-six years ago," Jenny said with awe in her voice. "How can your memory of that afternoon be so clear?"

"Because it was a day when someone I cared about was murdered. You tend to remember stuff like that," he said coolly. "It wasn't like it was just an ordinary Saturday."

Kyle remained on task. "Does your wife have an alibi for that day?"

For the first time, Doctor Burke looked angry. "My *wife* doesn't have anything to do with this."

"It's just a simple question," Kyle said. "Can anyone verify her whereabouts on that June afternoon in 1988?"

"She was in Philadelphia."

"That's not what I asked."

Shane sighed with defeat. "I'm sure somebody could vouch for her, but there's no reason for that. She doesn't have anything to do with this."

Kyle leaned back in his chair and said, "I'm assuming that your wife doesn't know about the affair you were having with Stella Jorgenson."

After a long pause, Shane conceded, "No, she doesn't know."

Looking at the doctor over his glasses, Kyle calmly posed, "Are you sure about that?"

"Very sure," Shane said without hesitation. "And she doesn't need to know about it, you got that?"

"Look, what goes on between you and your wife is certainly none of my business," Kyle said assuredly, "but solving this murder *is* my business. If there's any possible way you or your wife could have been involved in this crime, I need to investigate it…even if it does put a dent in your marital bliss. What I'm looking at is a very public outburst that exposed the affair that you were having with one of the nurses. It's quite possible that word could have gotten back to your wife, and she may have exacted her revenge on the other woman in your life."

"She didn't," Doctor Burke said adamantly. "So, I would appreciate it if you left my wife out of this."

Kyle remained calm, simply saying, "I will…for now." He reached into his wallet and pulled out a business card. "Listen, I'll leave you with this. I want you to think hard about that weekend… see if you can give me the name of someone who can verify you and your wife's whereabouts during the attack. Any information you can give us will be greatly appreciated."

Despite the tension during the conversation, the two men said amicable goodbyes; soon Jenny was back in the car with Kyle on their way to his office. "So, what do you think?" she posed. "Do you think he had anything to do with it?"

"It's too soon to tell," Kyle replied. He paused to listen to the directions his GPS was giving, turning the car in the direction he was supposed to go. "I will say the man appeared to be a bit of an asshole, pardon my French, but that doesn't necessarily make him a murderer."

Jenny slowly nodded as she looked out the window, silently wondering what Stella could have seen in Shane Burke—although, she quickly answered that question for herself. Doctor Burke was *someone*, which was all the young widow wanted at that point in her life.

"Oh," Jenny said as her train of thought reminded her of something she had wanted to tell Kyle. "I think I know why I've been getting all of my information from Nate instead of Stella herself."

"Oh yeah? Why is that?"

She leaned back against the headrest and glanced toward Kyle. "She wanted to be with her husband. He had been killed in a car accident a couple of years earlier; when she passed away, she got to be with him again." Jenny repositioned herself so she was looking out the front window. "Even though she had been taken violently, I think she was more concerned with seeing her husband again than she was with seeking revenge against her killer."

"She couldn't do both?" Kyle posed.

Jenny shook her head. "If her husband had crossed over, then she'd need to do the same in order to be reunited with him. Once a spirit crosses, they can't come back...and they can't communicate with me anymore, so I imagine that's why she's quiet."

Kyle nodded but didn't say anything.

In a strange way, Jenny felt happy for Stella. It was clear that she had missed her husband, and now she was able to spend an eternity with him. Although, Jenny concluded, nobody deserved the violent death that Stella had endured. The person responsible for that attack needed to be caught and punished, even if Stella herself wasn't suffering from unrest because of it.

"Do you know if there were any other deaths like Stella's around that same time frame?" Jenny asked. "Is it possible we're barking up the wrong tree by assuming she was an intended target?"

"I wasn't able to find any," Kyle assured her. "It was one of the first things I looked for. If there had been several cases like hers, that would have dramatically changed the nature of the investigation."

"That's what I was thinking," Jenny said. "I guess the fact that she was the only one means she was sought out deliberately."

"The overkill factor implies that, too. When a victim has as many stab wounds as Stella did, that usually means the attack was personal. The perpetrator didn't just want her dead—he wanted her to suffer."

Jenny thought about that notion for a moment. "Do you think either of the Burkes wanted her to suffer?"

"Honestly, if I had to guess, I'd say the Burke who was most likely want her to suffer would be Shane's wife Katherine," Kyle concluded. "I do want to avoid dragging her into this if I can. I'd hate to ruin a marriage unnecessarily." He let out a laugh. "I stick a fork in enough marriages in my line of work; I don't need to do it to another one. I do, however, want to interview that Colin kid—it sounds like he felt quite passionately about Stella, which means he may have been inclined to stab her eight times. Before we find him, though, I'd like to speak to some other people who were at that cookout...see if they have any feelings about what Colin's mindset may have been prior to the murder,,,or Doctor Burke's for that matter. Do you know who else was there that day?"

"No," Jenny confessed, turning to Kyle with a smile, "but I know where I can find that out."

Chapter 8

The dining room table was littered with papers and photographs. "It was cool of the cop to give you these," Zack noted as they tried to make sense of all the documents.

"I agree," Jenny replied. "I think he felt bad for the Minnicks."

"It's hard not to." After looking through a few pictures, Zack added, "You know, aside from the upside-down coffee table, it doesn't look like a murder took place in here."

"I know," Jenny said. "The carpet was brown, which hid the blood stains nicely. Trust me, though...when Nate knelt down beside her, his knees got soaked."

"I wonder if she died there or if she lived long enough to be taken to the hospital."

"I imagine she was alive when the paramedics arrived," Jenny commented. "If she had died at the house, they probably would have left her body there. Based on these pictures, she had been removed from the scene."

Zack shook his head. "That's horrible. I would like to think she'd have died more quickly than that."

"Don't think about it," Jenny said. "It's too upsetting." She scanned a document as a notion struck her. "Zack, what do you make of this? They said the murder weapon was a switch blade knife. But look..." She sorted through some pictures, pulling out one that had been taken of Nate at the police station. "Look what he was wearing."

Zack studied the photograph featuring Nate in a bloody t-shirt and a pair of brightly-colored nylon shorts.

"Correct me if I'm wrong," Jenny said, "but those shorts don't look like they'd have any pockets."

Squinting to get a better look, Zack noted, "It appears they don't."

"So, Nate would have had to either get the switch blade from Stella's house or carry it over with him in his hand. Nate's mother said he had been weeding the flower beds when he heard Stella scream…I doubt a switch blade would have been his tool of choice for that task."

"You wouldn't think," Zack said, "but you also said he wasn't very smart, right? Maybe he was using a switch blade to cut weeds."

Jenny exhaled. "Okay, so maybe that's not the silver bullet I thought it might be."

Ellen poked her head through the doorframe. "How's it going in here?"

"It's going," Jenny said. "There's so much information…it's a little overwhelming."

"Do you two want anything to drink?"

"I'm good," Zack said without looking up. "Jenny, you want something?"

Jenny smiled at Ellen. "No, thank you. I'm fine."

Ellen disappeared around the corner.

After silently looking through stacks of paperwork, Zack eventually said, "Huh. This is new."

"What is it?" Jenny asked.

"Look at this picture." He handed a photograph over to Jenny, who immediately noted a bloody handprint on a door frame.

"Oh my God," Jenny said. "Where is this from?"

"It looks like the sliding glass door, which is in the back of the house off the dining room."

"Holy shit," Jenny whispered, mostly to herself. "I guess it would make sense that the killer went out the back door if Nate didn't see him on his way in the front." She looked at Zack with awe. "Wouldn't this have been a big red flag to the detectives investigating the case? Willy Sanders said he saw Nate running out the *front* door with the knife...how could a bloody handprint have gotten on the door frame in the *back* of the house if Nate had been the killer?"

Zack shrugged. "That's why I showed you the picture."

Jenny was still stunned. "How could the detectives have overlooked this?" A flash suddenly appeared before Jenny's eyes. She could envision herself as Nate, running out the front door of Stella's house, heading toward the Minnick's. For the first time she noticed something was missing. "Zack," she said quickly, "are there any pictures of the outside of Stella's house?"

He looked around at the masses of papers around them. "Um...maybe? Why?"

"If I'm seeing it correctly, there was no car on the street. I would think if the killer had driven to the house, there would have been a car parked along the road...or at the very least a second car in Stella's driveway. I only saw one car in Stella's driveway, and I didn't see any cars at Nate's house."

The two scoured through pictures until they found some shots from the outside of the house. Just as Jenny had suspected, the only car to be seen was in Stella's driveway.

Jenny tapped her chin. "I wonder if Kyle will be able to tell us if that car was registered to Stella."

"I'm sure he can," Zack said.

"Okay, so is this evidence that Colin was most likely her killer? The Burkes didn't live close enough...if one of them had done it, they would have had to drive over, but it appears they didn't."

"I think it's either evidence that it was Colin or else one of the Burkes went over with the *intent* to kill Stella. If this was just a visit-gone-wrong from the Burkes, they probably would have parked in front of her house, not behind it. But, if murder had been the plan all along, it's reasonable to assume they would have gone through efforts to make sure their car wasn't visible to the neighbors."

"Let me see something," Jenny said as she pulled her laptop closer to her. She searched for an aerial view of Stella's old house, zooming out to see exactly where Colin's apartment complex fell with respect to her property. She turned the screen toward Zack, pointing to the parking lot that surrounded the apartments. "If the killer parked here, it looks like it would have been a short walk through the trees to get to Stella's house." She glanced up at Zack. "I wonder which of these buildings Colin lived in."

After studying the image, Zack replied, "I don't think it matters. Any one of those buildings would have been within walking distance."

She looked at the computer screen for another moment before holding up the picture of the bloody handprint. "It looks like the killer may have used this hand to brace himself as he pulled open the slider with the other. He could have run down the back deck and through the trees to the parking lot." She squinted at the photograph of the door sill before adding, "I wonder if they were able to lift any prints from this."

"If they did," Zack concluded, "I imagine it would have been difficult to explain why someone else's bloody fingerprints were at the scene of a crime Nate committed."

Jenny strummed her fingers on the table as she considered this piece of evidence. At that moment her phone rang; glancing at the caller, she noticed it was Megan.

"Hi Megan; thanks for returning my call."

"No problem," she said pleasantly. "What can I do for you?"

"Well," Jenny began, "I spoke to Doctor Burke today."

"Oh." Megan's tone was flat. "How did that go?"

"Interesting. He said that he had actually ended things with Stella a few days before she was killed."

"Really? I didn't know that."

"Stella hadn't mentioned that to you?"

"No," Megan confessed. "Honestly, we didn't talk about her love life that much. She knew I didn't really approve of what she was doing, and I think deep down inside she was embarrassed of it, so we never discussed it. She just did what she did, and I never said anything about it. That was kind of our unspoken agreement."

"Well, Doctor Burke said that after the cookout, Colin showed up at the ER and made a scene."

Megan let out a breath that revealed she had just conjured up a bad memory. "I had almost forgotten about that."

"Well, according to Doctor Burke, that confrontation led to a break up—between Doctor Burke and Stella, I mean. The private investigator I'm working with would like to speak to Colin about this, but before he does, he wants to hear from some of the other people at the cookout...you know, determine if they saw or heard anything that might suggest if Colin was capable of that level of violence." Jenny grabbed a pen and paper. "Can you tell me who else was there that day?"

"Sure. There weren't that many people there, though."

"Even better," Jenny remarked with a smile.

"Well, my ex-husband, who was my boyfriend at the time, was there. His name is Charlie Patterson." She went on to give Jenny his contact information. "His then-roommate was also there with his girlfriend. They're actually married now, so you can find them both together."

"And what are their names?"

Megan let out a laugh. "I'll spell it. They're Ed and Renee P-R-Y-Z-B-Y-C-K."

"Good grief. How do you say that?"

"Prez-be-yeck," Megan said; Jenny wrote down the phonetic spelling of their names as well as their phone numbers. "And that's it," Megan concluded. "That's everyone who was at the cookout."

"Well, this has been very informative," Jenny said with gratitude. "Thanks for your help."

"No problem," Megan said sincerely. "Please let me know if there's anything else I can help you with."

"You'll be the first to know." Jenny hung up the phone and showed the short list of the cookout's attendees to Zack. "Here it is," she said. "These are the only people who saw Colin and Doctor Burke together that day."

Zack studied the names, looking horribly confused. "What the hell kind of name is that?" He pointed to the Pryzbycks. "There aren't any vowels."

"Y can be a vowel," Jenny told him with a smile.

"Yeah, but only sometimes."

Jenny couldn't help but laugh; Zack's simplicity was definitely charming at times. She looked at him for a moment, studying his face, unable to deny the sudden and intense attraction she felt for him. She fleetingly wondered if having sex in Zack's parents' house would have been an acceptable thing to do.

"It's getting late," Zack said, glancing at his phone, snapping Jenny out of her little trance. "Do you think we should try to contact them in the morning?"

She shook her head quickly to rid herself of the thoughts she was having. "Probably," she replied, although she wasn't entirely sure what she had just agreed to do.

"My head is spinning," Zack confessed, "and I have to admit, I'm a little sore from renovating today. I'm not used to all this manual labor. I think I'm getting soft."

"You want to call it a night?"

"I want to have a beer and some chips—and then call it a night."

They scooted their chairs away from the table, and after a quick stop in the kitchen, joined Zack's parents in the living room.

"Well," Zack's father said from his recliner, "look who we have here."

Zack furrowed his brow as he sat on the couch, bowl of chips in hand. "What does that mean?"

"It just seems like it's about time you joined us, that's all."

Jenny could feel the tension starting to rise; she looked at Ellen, whose apprehensive expression provided confirmation.

"Dad," Zack protested, "I've been working."

"Since when do you spend twelve hours a day working?"

"Oh my God," Zack said with frustration. "My whole life you have always gotten on my case for not ever taking work seriously, and now that I have a job that I care about, you get on my case for working too much? I swear I can't friggin win."

Ellen interrupted with a loud exhale. "Can't we just drop this?"

"It would just be nice if you spent a little time with your mother, that's all," Andy said. "You haven't come to visit in a long time, and it seems to me that you've been ignoring her since you arrived."

Holding up her hand, Ellen said, "All I want is for the two of you to get along."

"Fat chance of that," Zack said bitterly.

Admittedly, Jenny felt uncomfortable; she wondered how Zack's mother had tolerated this behavior for the past few decades. It must have been unbearable to live with both of them before Zack moved into his own place.

An awkward silence ensued, interrupted only by sound of the sitcom on the television. Jenny felt painfully aware of her surroundings as she tried unsuccessfully to focus on the show; she was too afraid that another squabble was going to erupt at any moment. When Zack finished his snack and asked if she was ready for bed, she gladly bid his family goodnight and disappeared into the guest room.

Zack's obvious irritation only resurrected the attraction Jenny had felt for him earlier. He removed his shirt angrily, tossing it with vigor onto the floor and adding "My God, that man pisses me off so much."

Jenny bit her lip; Zack seemed painfully unaware of what was going through her head. She slipped out of her clothes and slid under the covers. "Come here," she said, lifting the sheet, inviting him to join her. "You look like you could use a little tension relief."

Zack sighed heavily as he climbed into bed. "I swear, I just can't do anything right in his eyes."

Jenny nestled into his shoulder and kissed his cheek a few times. "Okay, why don't you stop thinking about your father?"

Suddenly Zack seemed to become aware of what Jenny had in mind. "Hey, ho." He said with a smile. "What's going on here?"

She continued to shower him with kisses. "Do I really have to spell it out for you?"

"No, it's just unexpected, that's all."

"Do you want me to stop?"

"No," he said as he began to caress her back, "I most definitely do not want you to stop."

She pulled away and looked him in the eye with a smile. "Then stop talking."

Feeling satisfied, Jenny rolled over onto her back, sensing Zack glancing at her out of the corner of his eye.

"What was that about?" he asked.

She shrugged. "I don't know. You just looked good to me." She flashed him a toothy smile.

"I guess I should fight with my dad more often."

"No," she replied, "you should definitely *not* fight with your father more often. I had sex with you in *spite* of your argument, not because of it."

"You've got to admit, he makes it tough to be in the same room as him," Zack said. "He started harping on me the second I walked in there."

Jenny leaned up onto one elbow. "Do you know what I think might be going on here? I think your father's feelings might be hurt."

"What are you talking about?"

Jenny traced her finger in a circle on Zack's chest. "Well, that construction business of his means everything to him. It's like the family legacy—the one thing that Larrabee fathers pass down to their sons. It's been going on for generations… but you didn't want it. In fact, you hated it. You've said yourself that you were a lousy employee when you worked for him…maybe he just thought you were a lousy employee in general, but now he's seeing how dedicated you can be when you actually care about your job. Maybe he's wondering why you couldn't have cared this much about the family business that means so much to him."

"I hated the family business."

"I know," Jenny said compassionately, "and maybe he takes that personally."

"I think it's more a matter of him being disappointed in me."

"I don't know about that," Jenny reasoned as she collapsed onto her back and looked at the ceiling. "Have you ever given someone a gift that you thought was fabulous…only for the recipient to be a lot less excited about it than you were? That can be very upsetting."

"But he's acting like a jackass."

"Agreed," Jenny said. "I'm certainly not defending his actions…I'm just suggesting that his behavior may be less rooted in hate than you suspect it is. He might just be reacting negatively to your rejection of the family business...and if that's the case, he'd probably say this rift between the two of you is *your* fault."

"I'm sure he does think it's my fault," Zack grumbled. "To him, everything is my fault."

With a sigh Jenny determined she was entering into an argument she would never win. She hopped out of bed to brush her teeth and put on her pajamas, only to find Zack already asleep when she returned. She was so jealous of his ability to drift off that quickly; she always found her brain went into overdrive whenever she tried to sleep. Hoping this night would prove to be different, she climbed into bed.

Unfortunately, this evening ended up being just like all the others. Her mind began to race as she considered all of the pieces of the puzzle that just weren't fitting together. While the bloody palm print and the explosive scene at the emergency room seemed to implicate Colin, Doctor Burke certainly had more to lose if Stella had decided to betray him. Which of those men would have been angry enough to actually stab Stella eight times?

Getting nowhere, Jenny tossed and turned until she eventually managed to fall asleep. She hoped she would have a vision or a telling dream during the night, but she didn't find that to be the case.

"Thanks for breakfast, Ellen," Jenny said as she enjoyed her eggs. "I can't believe it's ten o'clock. I haven't slept this late in ages."

"You were tired," Ellen replied with a smile. "Being pregnant will do that to you."

"Honestly, I'm not even sure I can blame the baby for this one," Jenny said. "I have to admit that ever since I've entered my second trimester, I haven't had many symptoms. It's a bit ironic that as soon as I started to look pregnant, I stopped feeling pregnant."

"Were you sick in the beginning?"

"I felt sick, but I actually only physically got sick a few times. I mostly just walked around nauseated...and tired. Very, very tired. She certainly zapped my energy for a while."

"She?" Ellen said with surprise. "You know you're having a girl? I didn't think you were far enough along to tell yet."

"I'm not," Jenny replied as she stifled a laugh. "I just refer to the baby as *she* because Zack is so adamant that we're having a boy. Truthfully, I don't have any inclinations either way as to what gender the baby is. I just insist it's a girl to harass Zack."

Ellen pointed at Jenny. "I like you."

"He is convinced that Larrabees only make boys. Is that true?"

"Largely, yes," Ellen said. "I did manage to have a daughter, but Donna is one of the few girls born into this family in generations. Fortunately I have plenty of nieces—and now great-nieces—on my side to give me my girl fix, but on my husband's side it's all boys. Boys, boys, boys."

"That must make for some rough-and-tumble family reunions."

Ellen shook her head. "You have no idea. It's a miracle any of our houses are still standing."

"I guess it's a good thing your family is in the home-construction business," Jenny remarked with a smile.

"You're not kidding."

A short moment of quiet ensued, after which Jenny delicately said, "I started to talk to Zack last night...about his relationship with his father. I tried to get him to see things from your husband's point of view, but I wasn't very successful."

"Imagine that," Ellen said sarcastically.

Jenny's eyes drifted solemnly toward the table. "I do have to admit, I hate how much they fight."

"You and me both. Those two drive me crazy."

After thinking some more, Jenny posed, "Do you think there's anything we can do to get them to get along?" She hoped she wasn't overstepping her bounds when she added, "I would love for this baby to have a good relationship with her grandfather."

Ellen let out a little laugh. "Her. That's funny." She became more serious, however, when she said, "I would love that, too. I don't want to have to choose between spending time with my husband and spending time with my grandchild, but obviously things don't work out very well when you put Zack and Andy in a room together."

Resting her chin in her palm, Jenny said, "I wonder what we could do to get them to tolerate each other."

"I've been trying to figure that out for twenty-five years. Honestly, I thought if Zack ever got married and had a baby, that would do the trick," Ellen confessed. "Unfortunately, Zack came home already married to a woman we've never met...no offense...but that just adds fuel to Andy's fire."

Jenny was able to finish Ellen's sentiment. "That Zack can never do anything right."

"Exactly."

The jingle of Jenny's ring tone permeated through the room. "If you don't mind, I'm going to get that," Jenny said. "It might be about the case."

Ellen extended her hand toward the direction of the phone. "Go right ahead."

Zack was the caller. "Hey," Jenny said as she answered. "How's everything in renovation land?"

"Good, but I may want you to come out here," he said.

"Why...is something wrong?"

"No, nothing's wrong," Zack replied. "I just may have found something that can help prove Nate is innocent."

Chapter 9

Jenny arrived at Rob's house as quickly as she could. She had to park down the street due to all of the contractors' vans that clogged the end of the cul-de-sac. Walking eagerly to the door, she rang the bell; seconds later, Zack answered.

"What's going on?" she asked immediately as she entered the house and started up the steps.

"Well," Zack explained, "we pulled up the carpet and pad in the living room so we could put in the hardwood, and when we did, we saw a stain on the subflooring that I can only assume is blood."

Jenny had reached the top of the stairs at that point and was able to see the splotch Zack had been referring to, right where Stella had been in the visions. The pool was larger than she had expected. For a moment, she was immensely disturbed.

Zack continued, "That stain isn't surprising, but when we pulled up the carpet in the dining room that leads to the slider, we saw what looks like a trail of little blood droplets on the subflooring."

He walked Jenny over to the area in question, pointing downward. She did indeed see small, rust-colored circles in a path leading to the sliding door.

"And if you look over by the front of the house," Zack added, "you won't find any blood drops leading from the crime scene to the door that Nate ran out of."

With a furrowed brow, Jenny walked to the front of the house and verified what Zack had just said. The trail of blood clearly led out the back, ultimately to where the handprint had been. Confused, she looked up at Zack. "How do you think this will help clear Nate? We already knew the killer went out the slider."

"Well, here's what I'm thinking. Nate had gotten blood on him when he knelt down next to Stella, but none of that came off of him as he ran to the front door—at least, not enough to soak through the carpet and pad and stain the subflooring. But when the killer left, he left behind a trail of blood. I can't imagine that he'd gotten enough of Stella's blood on him to be dripping off of him like that. I can only assume that he had gotten hurt during the attack and this is *his* blood we're looking at."

Jenny covered her mouth with her hand as she considered the notion. Without saying anything else, she dialed her phone.

The greeting on the other end of the phone was abrupt. "Wilks."

"Hi, Detective Wilks, this is Jenny Larrabee." Secretly, Jenny was pleased she'd remembered her new name. "We've made a discovery at the house where Stella Jorgenson was killed, and it may help identify who her killer really was."

"Oh yeah? What did you find?"

Once again, Jenny found herself trying to quickly summarize something that could have taken forever to explain. With a sigh she began, "When we came to investigate this house, my husband noticed the current owner is in a wheelchair...but the house had carpet. My husband used to be in the home construction business, so he offered to replace the carpet with hardwood so the owner could get around more easily. When he pulled up the carpet and pad, he found a trail of blood on the subflooring that led to the back door. However, Nate was convicted based on testimony that he'd gone out the *front* door. My husband was thinking that it's too much blood for it to just be Stella's blood that had gotten on the killer...he thinks maybe the killer had gotten hurt during the attack and left a trail of his own blood."

"That often happens," Detective Wilks replied. "When a perpetrator stabs a victim multiple times, the knife can become slippery. Not only that, but if the blade hits bone, the knife stops moving and the perp's hand keeps going. That often leads to the perp's hand sliding down the blade, and he cuts himself as a result."

Jenny curled her lip at the thought but continued anyway. "I don't suppose there is any way you could come over here and investigate, is there?"

"Me, personally? No," Wilks said. "But I can send a forensics team out there for you."

"Can you?" Jenny asked. "That'd be great."

"Just try not to touch any of the stains until they get there," Wilks added. "I know it's been a long time, but the less contamination, the better."

Jenny grew tired of waiting for the forensics van to show up. A second visit to Willy Sanders' house had left her standing on the stoop again with no one answering the door. She had also reached a dead end when she'd called local hospitals, asking if they had any records of hands being stitched up the day Stella was killed. Hospital records didn't go back that far, and even if they did, doctor/patient confidentiality would have prohibited her from learning anything anyway. She put in a call to Kyle to see if he could investigate it more, but that still left her with nothing else to do in the meantime.

To be productive, she called Ellen and got the phone numbers of both Charlie Patterson and the Pryzbycks from her notes in the dining room. She figured she could at least have a discussion with the people who had been at the cookout before the murder while she waited. With the numbers in hand, she slipped out onto the back deck to make her phone calls.

She called Charlie first but had to leave a message. Next, she dialed the home number of the Pryzbycks, and a male voice answered. "Hello."

Assuming she'd gotten the husband, Jenny posed, "May I speak with Ed please?"

The man's reply was blunt. "Ed isn't here."

"Oh, well, may I speak to Renee please?"

"Yeah, hang on." She heard him call in the distance. "Renee! Phone's for you."

After a moment Jenny heard a woman's voice. "Hello?"

"Hi, Renee...My name is Jenny Larrabee. I got your number from Megan Patterson regarding the murder of Stella Jorgenson."

"Yes," she said with recognition, "Megan told me you might be calling."

"Well, I was wondering if I could ask you a few questions about what happened at the cookout the weekend before Stella was killed. I know you were there, as were both of Stella's boyfriends, and I was wondering if you had seen anything that might indicate which of them—if either—might have been angry enough with her to do such a thing."

"Sure," Renee said. "It's been a long time, but I'll do my best to try to remember. In fact, I've been thinking about it since Megan called me last night...I've been trying to recall some of the details of that day."

"Have you come up with anything?"

"Well," she began, "I do remember how angry Colin was when he first showed up. The doctor guy wasn't upset at first...it wasn't until Colin started demanding to know who he was that the doctor became elevated."

"Were any threats exchanged between the two of them?"

"No, I don't remember any threats. Insults, maybe, but not threats."

"How about after the guys became separated? After Colin left, did Doctor Burke say anything to you about him?"

"He did make one comment, although I can't remember exactly what he said. It was something to the effect of *a boy will never win if he tries to compete in a man's game*, or something like that."

"What about Colin? Did he say anything after he came back that night?

"He asked questions more than anything. He asked me if I knew exactly what the doctor was holding over Stella's head...what he was making her do to keep her job...that kind of thing. I remember feeling uncomfortable because it was obvious from her behavior that the doctor wasn't requiring Stella to do *anything* against her will—that was just something Stella had told Colin to explain why Doctor Burke was at the house."

"So, how did you respond to his questions?"

"I deferred, mostly," Renee admitted. "It wasn't that difficult to do. This was my first time meeting her. I had just started dating Ed then, and he only knew her because he was roommates with Megan's boyfriend. Megan usually hung out at his and Charlie's place...she didn't like to flaunt her boyfriend in front of Stella. This was the first time that I know of where Charlie and Ed actually hung out at Megan's."

"What was your impression of Stella?" Jenny asked.

"Um...well...I hate to speak ill of the dead, but I wasn't that impressed by her. I mean, she was nice and all, but she slept with two men in a single afternoon. I was a little put off by that, obviously, as was Ed. He actually made some comments about what a slut she was...not to her face, certainly, but afterward."

Jenny was unsure what to feel. She couldn't fault the Pryzbycks for having that opinion of Stella. However, knowing why she acted the way she did, Jenny felt genuine sympathy for her. This whole situation was just sad.

Jenny concluded the call with Renee and considered the information in front of her. If Colin sincerely believed that Stella had to perform sexual favors in order to keep her job, his fury certainly wouldn't have been directed at her...he would have wanted to exact his revenge on Doctor Burke.

But the trail of blood inside the house led out the back door, which faced the apartment complex where Colin had lived. It almost seemed like the path was being laid out to her killer.

Was it possible that Colin had discovered he was being duped and was angry at Stella for that? Angry enough to kill her?

Jenny let out a deep sigh of frustration. None of her questions would be answered while she sat in the house waiting for the forensics team to show up, and waiting was her least favorite thing to do.

The van finally arrived; a man and a woman in uniform emerged, carrying kits into the house. Zack and Rob greeted the detectives as Jenny remained quiet in the background.

After looking around, the female detective announced, "First we have to verify that these stains are actually blood."

"Does that mean you'll use Luminol?" Zack asked. He appeared proud of himself.

"Actually, no," the woman replied. "We would use Luminol to try to find blood that isn't visible to the naked eye. Since we can see this, what we want to do instead is run some tests to make sure it's human blood we're looking at."

She rubbed a wet cotton swab on the large stain in the living room, dripping a substance from a small bottle onto the tip, which immediately changed color. Holding up the swab, the detective added, "This spot is definitely human blood, and based on the amount of it, I would say it's a safe bet that this is where the victim was assaulted. I know she ultimately didn't survive her injuries, and a pool this large would be indicative of a fatal level of blood loss."

She bled to death, Jenny thought. *What a horrible way to go.*

"What about these littler spots over here?" Zack asked as he pointed. "These are the ones that lead me to believe the killer left out the back door, not the front door."

The detective raised her eyes to look at Zack. "I can test these spots for human blood, but there'd be no guarantee that these blood stains are from the same time period as the murder. Somebody could have had a nosebleed last year, and that would explain why there are drops of blood in a trail."

Zack looked a bit defeated as the woman tested the spots, which also resulted in a positive reading. "It is blood," she said. "Human blood." She gestured to her partner, who in turn walked over to her with a kit.

They proceeded to cut out little sections of the floor that had blood on it, both from the small drops and the larger stain. After bagging and tagging the samples, the forensics detectives started to pack their belongings.

"So, what now?" Zack asked.

"Well, next they will run a DNA analysis on the blood...but that will take a while. Once they get a profile, they will determine if the trail of blood came from someone other than the victim. If it did, they will compare it to the DNA of known criminals in the database. Even if they hit on a match, that wouldn't be a slam dunk...it would just mean that somebody with a criminal record has bled in this house." As she walked toward the front door, she added, "But it could at least give the lead detective a place to start looking."

Zack thanked the team and walked them outside. Jenny took the opportunity to follow the trail of blood to the slider door, looking out into the backyard, past the trees and to the brick building that sat a few hundred yards away. She could barely see the apartment building through all of the leaves, but she imagined in the winter time the view would have been much more direct. Although, she surmised, the murder took place in the summer, so the killer would have been able to hide relatively well in all the foliage. Perhaps those dense leaves provided sufficient cover for the killer to disappear without notice.

Zack returned into the house, and once again Jenny found herself overwhelmed by instant and inexplicable attraction to him. The fact that he was unaware of her sudden feelings made him even more appealing. He was just going about his business, and yet he looked very good to her. Perhaps they would need to have a little more alone time at his parents' house that night.

"Well, that was anticlimactic," he said sadly.

"Don't worry," Jenny replied as she went over and put her hand on his arm. "We'll get there. I'll go back to your parents' house and start looking through the documents again. We've only scratched the surface of those…maybe there's something hidden in there that will help."

He nodded, although his disappointment was still apparent.

"Hey, if it makes you feel any better, I don't think it looks like a nosebleed. I realize the detectives are required to interject doubt into every scenario, but I find it a little bit strange that a nosebleed would start right at the same spot Stella had been killed and the bleeder would head straight for the back door. If your nose was bleeding, or you had innocently cut yourself, why would you leave? Wouldn't you head for the bathroom or the kitchen to get a towel or something?"

"That's what I was thinking," Zack said.

She patted his back. "This may still pan out. It may take a while, but it might give us our answer." With a smile she added, "And by the way…the house is looking great."

"I don't get this," Jenny muttered as she once again studied the picture of the bloody handprint. "How could this have just been ignored?"

She set aside the picture as she began the more daunting task of looking through the written documents; there seemed to be a million of them. After thumbing through countless pages, she stumbled across a piece of paper that induced an undeniable wave of familiarity over her. Pulling that paper out of the stack, Jenny realized she was staring at a copy of the signed confession.

She covered her mouth with her hand as she began to read. Almost immediately, another wave washed over her, this time taking her back to that room at the police station she had visited with Detective Wilks. She was seated at a table with Sergeant Finneran standing on the other side, leaned over with his fists resting on the table. A cigarette burned between the fingers of Finneran's right hand; Jenny found herself irritated by the smoke. The sergeant looked angry, although she couldn't figure out why. Perhaps he was mad that she hadn't been able to call the police once she had gotten back to her house.

"So, why don't you tell me why you went over there today?" Finneran's Boston accent was thick.

"Over where?"

The sergeant seemed angered by the question; his response was unnecessarily loud. "To Stella's house."

"I heard Miss Stella scream. I thought she might have hurt herself."

"Uh-huh. Okay." Sergeant Finneran leaned in closer. "So why don't you tell me why you *really* went over there."

Jenny was confused. She had just answered that question. "Um...I thought Miss Stella was hurt."

Finneran took a drag of his cigarette and squinted. "So, you're telling me you went over there *after* she had already been stabbed."

"Yeah."

"Then why did you have a knife with you?"

"I found it."

"You found it?"

With a nod, Jenny said, "Yes."

"Where was it?"

"On the floor...next to Miss Stella."

"And you picked it up and used it to stab her, didn't ya?"

"No."

"No? What do you mean no?"

"I picked it up, but I didn't stab her."

"So, you found the knife at her house, and you picked it up, but you *didn't stab her*?"

"That's right."

Finneran stood up with frustration and paced a few moments. He sucked on his cigarette one more time before saying, "And why, exactly, would you do that?" He resumed his position of intimidation, leaning over Jenny at the table.

She wasn't sure how to answer, so she remained quiet.

"You don't have an answer for me, do ya? That's because you're not telling me the truth. You went over to her house with that knife, didn't ya?"

"No."

Finneran's voice became louder and even angrier. "Maybe you're not hearing me correctly. I said, you went over to her house with that knife in your hand, didn't ya?"

Jenny knew that for some reason she was supposed to say yes to the question, even though it wasn't true. Saying no was making this man angry, and she didn't want that. He was scaring her with how mad he was. "I guess."

"You guess? What do you mean, *you guess?*"

"I guess I brought the knife over."

With that, Finneran stood up and looked satisfied. "Now we're talking."

Jenny felt relief that he didn't seem angry anymore. She decided that just agreeing with him would keep him calm. For whatever reason, she was supposed to just say yes to whatever he said.

The vision faded, and Jenny found herself staring at the confession, still shaken by the Sergeant Finneran's intensity. As the immediate fear left her body, sadness took over. Nate Minnick, the boy who won the citizenship award—the boy who would have bought sand in a desert if he thought saying no would have been offensive—simply didn't want to upset the man who was interviewing him. Based on the amount of confusion she felt during the interrogation, Jenny figured it was a safe bet that Nate didn't know how much was at stake. He hadn't realized that by agreeing with the sergeant he was sealing his fate, and Jenny found that notion to be horribly upsetting.

She continued to read the confession, noting how many sophisticated words were weaved into the narrative. With an IQ of seventy-two, Nate wouldn't have known what a lot of those words meant. He simply signed on the bottom line to make his immediate life easier.

Ultimately, she focused on exactly what Nate had agreed to. The statement had said that Nate had gone to Stella's house with the switch blade and made sexual advances toward her. When she turned him down, he became angry and initiated an attack, stabbing her eight times in the back and chest.

Jenny noted the confession offered no explanation for how a bloody handprint would have gotten on the back door sill, nor did it state what on earth would have possessed Nate to suddenly go over there that day, knife in hand, and make sexual advances that he'd never made before. Considering Nate's IQ and the holes in the story, Jenny marveled at how this confession ever held up in court.

Before she made a stink, however, she wanted to make sure she had her facts straight. Reaching for the phone, she immediately dialed Megan. Fortunately, she was available.

After the typical pleasantries, Jenny stated the reason for her phone call. "I was just wondering how often Nate Minnick came over to your house to visit before the murder."

"How often he came over?"

"Yes," Jenny replied, "how many times did he knock on your door?"

"Never," Megan said, seeming somewhat surprised by the question. "I mean, he may have rung the doorbell when our mail got delivered to his house by mistake, but he never just came over for no reason."

"That's what I figured," Jenny remarked. "You didn't mention any visits when I spoke to you, and I imagine that you would have brought that up if it had been something that happened with any kind of regularity."

"You're right," Megan agreed, "I would have mentioned it."

Jenny thanked her for the information and ended the call. Unsure of whether she should have called Detective Wilks or Kyle, she decided to call the person who claimed to be less busy.

"Hello, Jenny," Kyle said when he answered. "What can I help you with?"

"I'm troubled," Jenny confessed.

"Troubled? By what?"

"Given his low IQ, I just don't see how the jury could have convicted Nate based on his confession, especially if you consider there was an unaccounted-for handprint on the back door."

"That's because you're young," Kyle said. "You grew up in the DNA generation. Back in the eighties, however, there was no such thing as DNA analysis, so the biggest factors in a slam-dunk investigation were a confession and eye-witness testimony…both of which were present in this case."

"But his confession was clearly coerced. There were words in that document that a person with a seventy-two IQ wouldn't have understood."

"I know you may find this hard to believe, but the notion of a false confession is a relatively new concept. Back when I was first starting out in this field, people took confessions at face value. It wasn't until the advent of DNA that law enforcement realized that sometimes people confess to crimes they didn't commit. Joe Psycho would swear up and down that he was the perpetrator, only for the DNA at the scene to prove he wasn't. It was mindboggling at first—nobody could figure out why someone would risk spending life in prison—or even the death penalty—if they hadn't committed the crime. More recent research has been able to provide us with some answers. Some people are looking for attention; others are mentally ill or, like Nate, mentally impaired. There's also the added dimension of sketchy interrogation techniques. Even a perfectly sane, intelligent individual can confess to a crime he didn't commit if the questioning is brutal enough. After hours and hours of being yelled at with no food, drink or bathroom breaks, even the most competent individual can give in and admit fault. They're that desperate for the interrogation to end."

Jenny scratched her head as she considered this information. "Do you think there is a videotape of this interrogation somewhere? Maybe if the right person sees it, they can determine that Nate's confession was unreliable."

Kyle's sigh gave away the fact that he was about to deliver bad news. "Unfortunately, back in 1988, interrogations weren't routinely videotaped. That, too, is a relatively new phenomenon."

While turning her face into a pout, Jenny said, "Then how are we going to show that this confession was coerced?"

The pause seemed to take forever. "I don't think you will." After more silence he added, "If you plan to exonerate Nate, I think your best bet will be to find who really did this."

Chapter 10

"Ed," Jenny said through the phone. "Thanks for returning my call."

"No problem," he replied. "Renee told me she's already spoken to you."

"Yes, she did earlier today. I guess you know the reason why I called you, then."

"I do," Ed replied. "You'd like to know if I saw or heard anything at the cookout that might point the finger at who did this. It turns out you may be in luck, actually."

Jenny's ears immediately perked up. "Oh?"

"Yep. I spent a good deal of time talking with Stella that day. Even though I had never met her before, it turned out she used to be one of my father's students at Braynard College. My dad taught Biology there for thirty years, and she took one of his courses as part of her nursing degree."

"It's a small world, huh?" Jenny asked.

"Well, it's a small town...with one college in it," Ed said with a laugh. "My father ran into people he knew every time he went out. I swear, everywhere we went, I'd always hear someone yell, 'Professor P!' I think his students really liked him, even if they couldn't say his name."

"Anyway," Ed continued, "Stella had a little too much to drink the afternoon of the cookout, so she ended up getting loose lips. She said things to me that you wouldn't ordinarily tell someone you'd just met."

Jenny was eager for him to get to the point.

"She explained that she worked with Doctor Burke, and at first she thought this thing she had going with him was cool, but she said he was starting to become overbearing—possessive—and that wasn't what their relationship was supposed to be about."

Jenny furrowed her brow; this did not align with what Shane Burke had said the day before. She wrote down the notes nonetheless. "So, *she* was getting fed up with *him,* that's what you're telling me?"

"Well, that's what *she* told *me*. Whether it's true or not, I don't know."

"Was Doctor Burke or Colin around when she said that? Do you remember?"

"I do remember. She said it when Doctor Burke was standing just a few feet away from us. She was being loud, too, due to the alcohol. I felt uncomfortable during the conversation because he was within earshot. That's why I'm able to remember it so well."

Nerves surged within Jenny; she couldn't help but feel like she was on to something. "Do you think he heard her?"

"If he did, he didn't let on," Ed replied. "But the girl did end up dead the following weekend."

Jenny thought back to her conversation with Doctor Burke; he claimed to be working the day of the murder. She determined she'd have to look into that claim to see if it was really true.

"What was your impression of Doctor Burke?" she asked.

"Cocky...just like you'd expect from a middle-aged man who cheats on his wife with twenty-somethings."

"Do you think he was capable of murder?"

Ed let out a sigh, apparently as he contemplated. "I can't say. I've never met a murderer before."

"Okay, then, let me switch gears. What was your impression of Colin?"

"I actually felt sorry for the guy. It was clear that he was easily manipulated. When Stella fed him that line of crap about the doctor using his position of authority to force her to date him, Colin fell for it hook, line and sinker. You know, he kind of reminded me of a puppy dog...he had that same allegiant-to-a-fault sort of quality about him."

"So, you would say he felt very passionately about Stella?"

"Oh, yes," Ed agreed, "without a doubt."

Jenny rubbed her eyes; she was still no closer to the truth. "Well, thank you very much for taking the time to speak with me."

"No problem," Ed replied. "Feel free to call any time you have questions."

"Thanks," she said. "I'll do that."

"I've heard from everyone except Charlie," Jenny explained to Kyle through the phone, ignoring the hunger that the smell of dinner was invoking in her. "Based on what Megan says about him, I'm not sure I will hear back from him. She says he's rather irresponsible."

"She's his ex-wife?" Kyle posed.

"Yup."

"Then you need to take her opinion with a grain of salt. If there's one thing I've learned at my job over the years, it's that."

"Well, so far it's proving to be true. I've gotten in touch with both Ed and Renee Pryzbyck, as well as Megan. It's just Charlie that's been elusive."

"Have Ed, Renee or Megan given you any information that looks like it will be helpful?"

"They all seem to imply that Doctor Burke had the motive but Colin had the passion. I'm really still back at square one."

Kyle maintained the calm demeanor that seemed to be ever-present with him. "Oh, well. It was worth a shot. Sometimes you can find some things out ahead of time that will give you a leg up when you interview a suspect. Other times, like now, you get nothing."

"So, when would you like to pay our friend Colin a visit?"

"How about tomorrow morning? He works as a loan officer; perhaps we can pay him a little surprise visit at his job."

"You like those surprise visits, don't you?"

"They're the best kind," Kyle explained. "There's no chance to rehearse your responses that way."

"Or to run," Jenny added.

"That's right," Kyle agreed. "Or to run."

The attraction Jenny had felt toward Zack earlier in the day had remained steadfast; she snuggled up onto his shoulder after they climbed into bed, caressing his chest gently with her hand.

"You'd better be careful," he warned. "If you keep this up, Little Zack is going to wake up, and then he's going to expect things."

Jenny smiled playfully. "I'd kind of like little Zack to wake up for a while."

With that, Zack looked at her in disbelief. "For real?"

"Yes, for real."

"Wow. I didn't think we'd be doing it in my parents' house at all, and here we are doing it for the second night in a row."

Liking the sound of what she'd heard, Jenny said, "Does that mean he'll come out and play?"

"Little Zack always wants to play," Zack replied as he rolled over on top of Jenny. "All he needs is an invitation."

"What do you have planned today?" Jenny asked as Zack climbed out of bed the next morning. She remained comfortable under the covers.

"Well, the chairlift guys are supposed to come, and we finally got approval from the county to begin the handicapped ramp in the front yard."

"What about the homeowner's association? Have they approved it?"

"They have to approve it. It would be a violation of the Fair Housing Act to tell a homeowner he can't put a handicapped ramp on his property because it's *unsightly*." He made finger quotes. "Rob can apply for approval after it's built; they can't say no. The county, on the other hand, wants to make sure the ramp is structurally sound, so they need to approve it before we begin."

Jenny shrugged. It sounded good to her. "A chairlift and the ramp; that's on your agenda for today?"

"Yup. That, and starting the bathroom. How about you? What are you working on?"

Jenny glanced at the time. "Well, I'm going with meet with Kyle so we can ambush Colin at work. Then after that, who knows? It will all depend on what Colin has to say."

Zack walked over to the bedroom window and peeked out the blinds, looking elated by what he saw.

"What has you so happy?" Jenny asked.

"My father's car is gone. He's already left for work, so I can have a pleasant morning."

"Seriously...you two are like toddlers."

"Nuh-huh," Zack said in his most child-like tone.

Jenny rolled her eyes; for some reason she did love that man. Once again feeling an insatiable need to be with him, she lifted up the covers and said, "Do you want to come back to bed?" She smiled at him flirtatiously. "That way you can have a *really* pleasant start to your day."

Zack looked stunned. "What has gotten into you?"

With a giggle, Jenny confessed, "I don't know. I've just been in the mood a lot lately."

Zack's eyes became wide as saucers. "I know what's happening." He pointed at Jenny as he approached her. "You have a penis!"

With a laugh, she looked down her body and replied, "Last I knew, I didn't."

"No, not *on* you. *In* you." He moved the tip of his finger from Jenny's face to her belly. "That baby has a penis. Don't you see? You've got a penis and you have extra testosterone and now you know what it's like to be a guy and be totally horny all the time and now you want it twenty-four hours a day." He spoke all in one breath, ending his statement with an emphatic folding of his arms across his chest.

Jenny bit her lip and grinned. "You really think that's what's happening?"

"It's got to be. There's no other explanation for it." He tumbled back into the bed. "The tables have totally turned. Now *you're* the horny one." He pursed his lips in feigned snobbishness. "I ought to say no to you just so you know how it feels to be shot down."

Still laughing, she posed, "Wouldn't that be cutting off your nose to spite your face?"

"Yes, but I think it would teach you a valuable lesson."

"And what lesson would that be?"

"It would teach you to be compassionate towards men and their stupid behavior, which is almost always sexually motivated."

"That's not really a lesson."

"You, my little wife, are splitting hairs...in what I believe is a failed attempt at dodging the issue. In the past you have routinely expressed disappointment in the inner workings of the heterosexual male brain, and now—in a cruel twist of fate—you get to experience what it feels like to be one."

Jenny leaned up onto one elbow and looked at Zack. With her best male voice, she primitively said, "So, does this mean we're not gonna do it?"

Zack thought about it for a moment. "Aw, what the hell." He flipped over onto Jenny and began to kiss her.

Kyle flashed his identification. "I'd like to speak with Colin Barrymore, please."

The secretary looked intimidated. "He's with a client right now, but I can have him talk to you when he's done."

"That would be great, thank you."

Kyle and Jenny took a seat in the lobby. She turned to him and asked, "Aren't you worried about putting his job in jeopardy?"

He shrugged and shook his head. "Nah. He's not a suspect at this point, but he was dating a young woman that got murdered, so he does need to be questioned. I can explain that to his boss if I need to, but the whole *Holy-shit-these-guys-showed-up-at-my-job* notion might throw him just enough to get a little extra honesty out of him."

After a short wait, a man in a suit escorted a couple out of his office. He had red hair and a round, boyish face, giving him a distinct look of innocence that immediately struck Jenny. She couldn't imagine him plunging a knife into a woman he loved eight times, although Jenny knew she had to get that thought out of her head. Looks most certainly could have been deceiving, and a childlike face did not necessarily mean he wasn't capable of terrible things.

Kyle stood up and approached the man. "Colin Barrymore?"

"Yes," he replied, looking both friendly and confused.

"Kyle Buchanan." He once again flashed his identification. "May I have a word with you inside your office?"

Jenny's eyes flashed to the secretary, who looked like she had just seen a ghost, making Jenny wonder whether or not their interrogation tactics were sound.

Still looking dumbfounded, Colin agreed, inviting Kyle and Jenny to take a seat at his desk. "You may want to close the door," Kyle warned.

Colin heeded the advice, and the look on his face went from confused to almost fearful. He walked around his desk and took a seat, holding on to his tie as he did. "What can I help you with?"

Kyle began his explanation. "I'm looking into the murder of Stella Jorgenson back in 1988."

"Stella?" He looked back and forth between Kyle and Jenny. "That's what this is about?"

"Yes," Kyle replied, "we have reason to believe an innocent person was convicted of the crime."

In what appeared to be an a-ha moment, Colin sat back in his chair and widened his eyes. "It was that doctor, wasn't it? The one who was forcing Stella to date him so she could keep her job."

Jenny's heart bled for the man who apparently still believed—after all this time—that Stella was being honest with him.

"We don't know that for sure," Kyle said. "We're still looking into all possibilities at this point."

Colin seemed to ignore Kyle's comment. "You know, I suspected him. Even when they said the neighbor did it, I wondered if they had gotten it wrong. That doctor was obviously a jerk."

Opening his notepad, Kyle asked, "Did the doctor do or say anything specific that leads you to believe he played a role in her murder?"

Colin's shoulders sank and his expression became sad. "No, but I'm afraid I may have played a role in what happened to Stella."

"What do you mean by that?"

"I went to see him," Colin admitted. "A few days before Stella was killed, I went to the emergency room where the doctor worked, and I let him have it. I told him I would go to his bosses and let them know how he was using his position of authority to manipulate Stella into doing what he wanted her to do. Then I noticed the man was wearing a wedding ring." Colin looked appalled. "Can you believe it? *A wedding ring.* He was *married.* That's when I lost it and told him I would go to his wife with what I knew if he didn't leave Stella alone."

Kyle calmly jotted down the notes. "And you said this happened when?"

Colin looked like he could cry. "A few days before she was killed. When I first heard she'd been murdered, I thought for sure the doctor had done it...and he'd done it because of what I'd said. I felt so guilty. But then I found out it was the neighbor and the attack was random." His shoulders sank even further. "That made me feel less guilty, but it didn't help me miss her any less."

Jenny could fully understand Ed's puppy reference.

"Did you end up telling his wife about the...relationship...between Stella and Dr. Burke?"

Looking ashamed, Colin admitted, "I left a message on their answering machine."

Jenny and Kyle looked at each other with just their eyes.

"I was angry," Colin continued. "I realize I probably shouldn't have done it, but Stella deserved better, and so did this guy's wife, even though I'd never met her."

"What, exactly, did this message say?"

Letting out a sigh that showed he wasn't proud of himself, he admitted, "It just said that his wife might want to be aware that he has been forcing one of his nurses to become romantically involved with him so she can keep her job."

"I assume you have no way of knowing whether the doctor or his wife heard this message?" Kyle posed.

Colin shook his head. "I don't know who heard it."

"Well, that definitely puts an interesting spin on things," Kyle noted under his breath.

"Does this mean you are trying to prove it was him?" Colin posed eagerly. "Although, he must be in his sixties by now. He was my age, I think, when all of this went down."

"He is older now, yes," Kyle said, "but we're not necessarily trying to prove it was him. We're simply trying to find out who it was."

Colin scoffed. "You don't need to look any further than that guy."

"What if I said there was a trail of blood that led out the back door of Stella's house?" Kyle posed. "The door that someone most likely would have used if they left the scene and went to the apartments where you lived at the time of the murder."

He looked back and forth between Kyle and Jenny as if he didn't understand what was being laid out in front of him. "You think the killer lived in my building?"

"That's where the physical evidence points," Kyle said.

Colin looked as if his mind had been blown. "I wonder who it could have been, then."

Jenny felt deeply sorry for this man, who didn't seem like he was all that bright, at least not when it came to the ways of the world.

"Well, I can come up with one person who lived in your building who felt passionately enough about Stella to do this to her."

"Who?" Colin demanded, looking as if he wanted to find this person and wring his neck.

"Um…you, Mr. Barrymore."

"Me? Are you kidding? I never would have hurt Stella. I loved her."

"Exactly," Kyle reasoned. "You loved her, and you discovered the weekend before that she was dating someone else."

"Yeah, because she had to in order to keep her job."

"You believe that, Colin?" Kyle asked.

"Of course I do. It's the truth."

In a move that made Jenny feel grateful, Kyle simply nodded and accepted that statement. She saw no need in dashing Colin's idyllic image of Stella twenty-six years later.

"Just so we can eliminate you from the suspect list, can you provide us with an alibi who can verify your whereabouts the afternoon Stella was killed?"

"I was home then," Colin said. "I was by myself." He looked down. "I always thought that if I had just paid her a visit that day, none of this would have ever happened."

"Were you on the phone with anyone during that time frame?"

"I don't remember. It was a long time ago."

Kyle jotted the information down and closed his notebook. Standing up, he extended his hand, which Colin shook. "Well, Mr. Barrymore, we may be back in touch if any information warrants."

"Hey…let me ask you something," Colin said. "What makes you think the guy next door didn't do it?"

Kyle curled his lip into a half a smile. "A little birdie told me."

Jenny turned to Kyle as they drove back to his office. "I have a difficult time believing it was him," she confessed. "He just seems far too naïve to be a murderer."

"You'd be surprised," Kyle replied. "I've seen some strange things in my years as a private investigator."

Jenny thought back to some of her earlier cases and was once again reminded that looks could be deceiving. Still, she just couldn't see Colin doing something so horrific. "What do you make of that phone message? Do you think Katherine Burke heard it?"

"We may have to ask her," Kyle said, glancing at Jenny out of the corner of his eye.

"I'm with you on that. As much as you didn't want to drag her into this, I think we might need to."

"I'd like to catch her at a time when she isn't with her husband, though. I don't want him interfering with the questioning or influencing any of her answers. I would also like to avoid telling her in advance that we're coming, for the same reasons I wanted to avoid telling Colin. This may take a little research on my part. I have to figure out if she has any routines that would let us be able to anticipate her whereabouts."

Jenny leaned back in her seat. "Let's just hope that she does."

Jenny approached Rob's house to find Zack struggling with his end of an auger. She could tell the ground was hard as a rock; both Zack and a large misfit contractor were having a difficult time getting the machine to bore the hole that would soon house the footing for the handicapped ramp. As Zack maneuvered the machine, his triceps bulged out from under his shirt, which was drenched in sweat. Suddenly, Jenny found herself having another one of her urges.

She placed her hand on her belly; was this really evidence that she was having a boy? Was this what testosterone did to people? Did men really feel like this all the time? She stopped to consider how difficult that must have been to deal with. Perhaps she'd been a little tough on the guys she'd known throughout her life. Maybe they couldn't help their juvenile, sex-obsessed behavior.

At that point, Zack saw her and gestured a hello with his head. She smiled and waved in return, trying to tuck her poorly-timed attraction into her back pocket. Once he and his partner had stopped digging the hole, he set the auger down and walked over toward Jenny.

"How's it going?" she posed.

"Great. You should go inside and sneak a peek at the hardwood; it looks really good."

Jenny smiled lovingly at him. "I'll definitely do that."

"Did you get anywhere with the investigation?"

"Well, we found out that Colin had not only chewed Doctor Burke out in the ER, but he also left a message on their home answering machine in an attempt to tell Katherine about the so-called workplace sexual harassment. It's distinctly possible that his wife had discovered the little affair just before Stella was killed."

"Wow. That's pretty telling."

"That's what we're thinking. Kyle is trying to figure out her schedule so we can find a time to interview her when she will be by herself."

"Good work," he said with a smile that sent a tingle throughout Jenny's body. He wiped the dripping sweat from his forehead with his shirt, forcing her to look away before the feeling got out of hand.

"Well," she said uncomfortably, "I think I'll go inside and check out that hardwood."

"It's purdy," Zack said. "The guys did a good job."

She didn't look at him as she headed up the front steps, nor did she knock when she got to the front door. Upon looking through the glass, she noticed the chair-lift workers were in the foyer, and presumably they'd been in and out all day. One more person coming in shouldn't have been a problem, and she didn't want to interrupt Rob while he was working.

She headed up the stairs, smiling at the workers as she squeezed her way through. When she got to the top, she was greeted by a beautiful and shiny dark brown hardwood floor. The color resembled that of the carpet that was present while Stella lived there, and the sight of it elicited an undeniable wave of familiarity within Jenny.

She closed her eyes and the carpet returned, along with the floral couch and the overturned coffee table with papers sticking out from underneath. Stella lay on the floor as Jenny knelt next to her, grabbing her shirt, looking as if she was desperate to speak. Pulling Jenny in close, she was able to muster a few whispery words.

"Look for the son."

Chapter 11

"The way I see it, it could mean two different things," Jenny told Zack, who sat in the shade on the front steps with a glass of ice water. "She could either be referring to a child of the Burkes, or she might even be talking about Ed Pryzbyck."

"Ed Pryzbyck? Why would that mean him?"

Jenny sat next to Zack to avoid the heat. "Ed had mentioned that his father had been Stella's professor at Braynard College. They discovered that little tie-in during the cookout, when she was drunk and talking to Ed. If she was anything like me, she'd probably forget that his name was Ed, but she'd remember that he was Professor P's child, which is why she would have told Nate to *look for the son.*"

"Holy shit," Zack said before taking a big gulp of water. "That would be crazy, wouldn't it, if it was him?"

"It's crazy no matter who did it."

"Let me ask you this," Zack began. "What motive would Ed have had?"

"Maybe the same motive they claim Nate had. Maybe he had come over her house to get..." Jenny wasn't sure how to finish the sentence considering there were other people within earshot.

"Lucky?" Zack suggested with a smirk.

"Yes...he wanted to get *lucky*, and when she said no, he snapped."

"Okay," he replied, "but let me play the devil's advocate here. Ed was dating Renee at that point. I would think that if he wanted to go on a booty call, he'd have gone to her house."

"Well, Renee said they were new back then. Perhaps they hadn't reached that point in their relationship yet." Jenny thought of her own hard-to-ignore, deep-rooted urges the past few days. "Maybe Ed's libido got the best of him, and he thought Stella would be the way to go." She hated to admit this next part, but she had no choice. "After all, Stella had slept with two men in the same afternoon while Ed was there that day. Perhaps he thought she'd be an easy score."

Zack thought about it while he drained the rest of his water. "That's fair. You should look into his criminal record...see if he has a history of violence."

"Actually, *Kyle* should look into his background," she replied with a smile. "I was also thinking he could find out if our friend Doctor Burke and his wife have a son. Maybe *he* heard the answering machine message and decided to take matters into his own hands."

"Or the wife could have put him up to it."

Jenny nodded slowly. "Or Katherine could have put him up to it."

Commotion from inside the house caused Jenny and Zack to both turn around. Through the glass door, they could see Rob's two little girls cheering as the chair went up and down the metal railing. Zack looked over at Jenny. "I guess the chairlift guys are done."

With that, they both stood up and walked through the door into the foyer. One of the workers was telling Rob how to work the lift. "You just push this button here, and the chair will go down. Push this button, and it will go up."

Rob nodded in acknowledgement before turning to his bright-eyed children. "You two want to ride on it, huh?"

Both girls jumped and cheered excitedly.

The worker laughed and said, "They always do. It loses its appeal quickly, though, when they figure out how slow it goes. It's faster to sit on the top step and slide down on your bottom."

"Like this?" the older daughter asked, sitting down and scooting down the stairs at lightning speed, making a thud every time her rear end hit a stair. Jenny's butt hurt just watching her.

"Yes," the worker said pleasantly, "like that. You'll be able to go down the stairs much faster that way than anyone who uses the chair."

"Can we still do it, Daddy?" the younger one asked with wide eyes. The older daughter eagerly climbed back up the stairs.

"Sure thing. Hop on in." Both girls managed to sit in the chair together, but they argued over who got to push the buttons. Rob settled the dispute by telling one daughter she could push the down button and the other girl could press it on the way up.

Jenny smiled inside. These were the kinds of squabbles she'd hopefully have to address in a decade's time, and she couldn't wait.

The girls giggled and squealed as they traveled at a snail's pace up and down the stairs. The worker turned to Rob and said, "Don't worry. There's a call button at all three levels...the top, bottom and middle. If your girls decide to take the chairlift downstairs and you're upstairs, you can just press this button right here..." The man referred to a small green circle at the top of the steps. "Then you'll be able to bring the chair to you."

The smile on Rob's face spoke volumes. "This is amazing, thank you." He turned to Zack and Jenny. "And thank *you*. This will make my life immeasurably easier."

Jenny smiled genuinely. "Glad we could help." Then she looked at the sweaty man next to her who had been doing all the work, and suddenly she felt bad about being the one to reply. She patted Zack on the back, quickly regretting that decision when her hand became wet from his sweat. She wiped it discretely on her shorts.

Just as the man had indicated, the girls quickly became bored with the painfully slow chairlift and resumed the game they had previously been playing, which was to see who could slide the farthest in their socks down the new hardwood hallway. At that point, Rob took his inaugural ride on the lift; he nearly looked moved to tears.

Between the giggling girls and the clearly touched man, Jenny was finding this to be too much to handle. Tears were threatening, so she excused herself and made a phone call to Kyle on the front steps.

She described her latest vision to him. "Wow," he said. "I'll have to see if the Burkes have any sons, and if they do, how old they would have been at the time of the murder."

"Good point," Jenny said. "I don't think an eight-year-old would have committed this crime. We might also want to focus a little more on Ed Pryzbyck." She explained the connection between Stella and Ed.

"This is all very good stuff," Kyle said. "I think you may have just narrowed down the suspect pool substantially."

Jenny noticed a car pulling up to the house. "Let's hope so," she replied as she squinted to get a better look at the driver.

"I'll get on this right away. Oh, but before I go, I should tell you that Katherine Burke belongs to a few charitable organizations that have regular meetings. We ought to be able to contact her outside of one of those."

"Perfect," Jenny said, although she was only half paying attention. She was too busy focusing on the newest guest, whose identity was now known to her but whose welcome remained questionable.

She finished her phone call with Kyle and headed down the front steps, being careful to avoid the freshly-dug holes. "Andy, I'm surprised to see you here."

"I'm sure Zack will be, too," Zack's father said as he approached, glancing at the upturned soil. "Is this for a handicapped ramp?"

"Yes, sir."

He looked at the front steps and back at the holes. "He's not making it long enough."

Oh dear, Jenny thought, *and so it begins.* Unsure of what to say, she remained quiet.

"Is Zack inside?" Andy posed.

"Yes, sir. He's in there wrapping things up with the chairlift guys."

Without another word, Andy walked into the house.

Jenny didn't know what to do. She hated the idea of Zack being ambushed by his father, but her presence inside wouldn't have done anything to prevent that. Would Zack have felt better if she were in there giving him silent support, or would he have preferred that she not see the inevitable bickering that was about to ensue? She chewed on a fingernail as she considered her options.

It turned out she didn't need to decide. The front door opened, and Zack walked out telling his father, "That's because I'm not done digging yet, Dad. I took a break when Jenny got here. I'm perfectly aware of the code, and I promise the ramp will be long enough."

"What material do you plan to use?"

Somehow Jenny knew there was no correct answer to this question.

"Composite," Zack replied. "It's less maintenance than wood."

"Seems like there'd be less traction, don't you think?"

Zack looked at Jenny with eyes that said *I'm going to kill him.* Turning to his father he asked, "How did you know I was here?"

"Your mother told me."

"Remind me to thank her for that when I get home."

Jenny bit her lip to keep from laughing.

"I thought you might want a little help; that's why I came out."

"Well, I'm actually fine. We're making good progress, and I think Rob is pleased with the results so far."

Jenny heard her phone chirp, so she pulled it out of her pocket and looked at the screen. The message was from Kyle.

The Burkes have a son named Trevor who was 23 at the time of the murder.

She looked up at Zack and waved her phone back and forth. "I think I may have to get going."

Eager to get away from the bickering Larrabees, Jenny made the return phone call from her car. "So, what do you think is our best plan of attack?" she asked Kyle.

"Well, Trevor lives about an hour away from here. We could make a little trip and surprise him with a visit if you'd like."

Checking the time on her dashboard, Jenny noted she'd most likely be back in time for dinner if they left right away. "That sounds good. Won't he be at work right about now?"

"Maybe. I know he works as a manager of a home improvement store, so he may not work your traditional nine-to-five. But if you have the time, we can try both his workplace and his home and hopefully he will be at one of those two places."

"As it turns out," Jenny replied, "I've got nothing but time."

A man with salt-and-pepper hair answered the door of his well-maintained, average-sized home. Jenny assumed this was who they were looking for due to his striking resemblance to Shane. "Can I help you?"

Kyle showed his identification. "My name is Kyle Buchanan, and this is my partner Jenny. I'm a private investigator looking to speak with Trevor Burke, if he's available."

The man looked confused and apprehensive. "I'm Trevor Burke."

"Great," Kyle said professionally. "I'd like to ask you a few questions about a murder that happened in Mumford Springs back in 1988, if you don't mind."

Trevor's expression didn't change. "You mean that nurse who worked with my father?"

"That's the one. Would you be willing to speak with us for a little while?"

"Sure," Trevor said as he stepped back and gestured with his hand. "Come on in."

Jenny and Kyle walked through the front door, where she immediately noticed that, in contrast to his parents' house, Trevor's place wasn't very extravagant. It was nice, certainly, but rather understated; in her mind, this place felt more like home.

Once they were situated at the kitchen table, Kyle opened his notepad and began his series of questions. "The woman who was murdered was named Stella Jorgenson. Had you ever met her?"

"A few times," Trevor said plainly. "I think she was dating my father."

With that, Jenny looked over at Kyle, who in turn raised his eyes to meet Trevor's. "What makes you believe that?"

Trevor smiled and shook his head. "Because my father was very bad at being secretive. That, and he pretty much made a career out of dating every attractive twenty-something he could." The look on his face reflected a hint of disgust.

This was new to Jenny; she silently questioned whether Katherine Burke would have targeted Stella if she was only one of many mistresses.

Kyle remained focused on the issue at hand. "When did you meet Stella?"

"I ran into her a few times, so it's hard for me to say which of those meetings was the first. I know there was one time when I was irritated with my roommate, so I decided to stay at my parents' house for the weekend...unbeknownst to them. I walked through the front door to find my dad and Stella all cozied up on the couch together, drinking wine in front of the fireplace. They claimed they were just discussing work-related things, but I knew better." Trevor let out a laugh. "Any idiot would have known better."

Kyle scribbled furiously. "What happened at that point?"

Trevor smiled with only one side of his mouth. "I decided to be a jackass. I popped some popcorn in the microwave and cracked open a beer, joining the two of them in the living room. I turned on the TV, sat in the recliner and put my feet up, knowing full well I was being a third wheel. I didn't feel bad about that...don't to this day. What kind of son would I have been if I made myself scarce so that my father could cheat on my mother?"

"I'm certainly not judging," Kyle said in his typical cool demeanor. "What was their reaction to your presence?"

"They scooted a little further from each other on the couch and pretended to talk shop." Trevor shook his head. "I think they were under the impression that they had actually fooled me. I'm not quite sure how stupid my father thought I was, but apparently he didn't give me very much credit."

"Did you ever give your father any indication that you knew about his affairs?"

"No, not directly, but if he thought about it for a minute, he probably would have figured it out. As soon as I realized he was cheating on my mother, my attitude toward him became even worse than it already had been."

"How old were you when you figured it out?"

Trevor gave the question some thought. "I don't know. Mid-teens, I guess? As soon as I became old enough to stay home alone, my father started going out on the nights my mother was out of town. Initially, I wondered where he was going; I found it strange that he always had places to go when my mother wasn't around, but then he'd stay home when she was in town. It didn't take a whole lot of time for me to figure out he was doing something she wouldn't have approved of."

"When did you figure out it was affairs?" Kyle asked. "How did you know it wasn't gambling or strip clubs?"

"At first I didn't know, but we'd get these phone calls where the person would hang up after I answered. This was a time before caller ID and all that, so I couldn't see who was calling, but one time I picked up the phone in my room the same time my father picked up the downstairs phone. Before I had a chance to say anything, I heard him say hello. Of course I stayed on the line to eavesdrop on their conversation—I wanted to figure out what he had been up to all those nights. Well, the woman on the phone said her name was Danielle and she asked if they were *still on* for that night. It was that moment when I realized what my father's mystery plans had been all those times."

Jenny felt bad for Trevor; that must have been a terrible discovery for a kid to make.

Kyle, however, remained emotionless. "You said your relationship with your father became *worse* after that...meaning it wasn't very good to begin with?"

"My relationship with my father was bad from the moment my mother's pregnancy test came back positive." Jenny could detect a good deal of resentment in his tone. "Have you done the math? Do you know how old my father was when I was born?"

"According to my calculations, he was eighteen," Kyle stated. Jenny looked at him, wondering why he hadn't mentioned that earlier.

"Yup. Eighteen when I was born; seventeen when I was conceived. I have accident written all over me. Mind you, my father did the honorable thing and married my mother, but I don't really think he wanted to. He was just a man who was overly concerned about his image, so he didn't want to come off looking like a rat."

"It didn't stop him later," Jenny said before her filter had the chance to operate. "He wasn't afraid to look like a rat when he was cheating on his wife in his forties."

Trevor turned to Jenny, and she couldn't help but notice he had many of the same mannerisms and facial expressions as his father. She wondered if he realized that.

With a scoff, Trevor replied, "Oh, believe me, my father was still very much concerned with his image then. That's why he only went out with younger women...*attractive* younger women."

Jenny was a bit surprised. "*All* of his mistresses were younger?"

"All the ones I saw were," he said with repugnance. "You know, I was eventually able to figure out who that Danielle person was. I knew she had sounded young on the phone, but it wasn't until a few weeks later that I realized she was my friend's older sister. I think she was twenty or twenty-one, maybe? And my dad was, like, in his thirties."

"How did you find out who she was?" Jenny asked.

"I was hanging out at the mall with my friends." Trevor let out half a laugh. Holding up his hand, he explained, "I know, but it was the eighties. I was fifteen. Hanging out at the mall was the thing to do."

"I remember," Kyle said without expression. "I was there too. It's where the girls were."

"Exactly." For once Trevor actually smiled. "But anyway, I was at there at the mall when I noticed my father in a lingerie store with my friend's older sister...*Danielle*. That's when I put two and two together." Disgust once again gripped his face. "Do you know how mortifying that was?"

"Was your friend with you? Danielle's younger brother?"

"No," Trevor replied, "not that day, thank God. And none of my other friends noticed them, so I just directed the group to hang out somewhere else." He shook his head. "I was the only one to see them, but it was still humiliating."

A thought occurred to Jenny. "What was Danielle's last name?"

"Church," Trevor said. "Ironically."

"You said there were other mistresses." Kyle asked, continuing his line of questioning. "Do you know about how many?"

Trevor thought about the question but ultimately said, "I'm not sure. I left for college when I was eighteen, so he probably went hog-wild after that. Who's to say how many women he ended up with?"

Kyle took a moment to review everything he'd written down. "Do you know how long your father's relationship with Stella lasted?"

"Longer than the others," Trevor replied, "although I'm not sure exactly how long. All the other women—or should I say *girls*—had a pretty rapid turn-around, as far as I could tell, but I already knew Stella was dating my father at the Christmas party my father threw at the house." He leaned back in his chair and shook his head. "It was so disgusting to see her having a pleasant little conversation with my mother, telling her how delicious her hors-d'oeuvres were, when she was regularly sleeping with my father."

"Do you think your mother suspected there was an affair going on?" Jenny asked. Her heart ached for Katherine.

With a shrug, Trevor replied, "If she did, she didn't let on."

"Okay, so they were already dating at Christmas," Kyle proclaimed without looking up from his notepad, "and they broke up the week before she was killed in June…so the relationship lasted at least six months?"

"Sounds about right. Like I said, that was long for my father. As far as I can tell, there must have been something *special* about Stella." He rolled his eyes, his annoyance still evident after all these years.

"You said you ran into her *a few times*," Kyle said. "Did you ever have any interactions with her? By that, I mean conversations beyond your typical hello."

"No. She repulsed me, really. She and every woman like her."

Kyle looked up with just his eyes. "You mean every woman who had an affair with your father?"

Shaking his head, Trevor elaborated, "No, every woman who didn't have the sense to recognize a decent man when she saw one. My father was such an obvious schmoozer, yet all these beautiful young women fell for his BS. Meanwhile, guys like me who had honest intentions weren't given the time of day. It would have been fascinating to watch if it hadn't been so infuriating. I mean, why would these women prefer to be with an old, *married,* smooth-talking womanizer when they could have been with someone who genuinely cared about them? It was absurd."

"Because they were young and dumb," Jenny found herself saying, surprising herself with just how much she sounded like Zack. "Young women tend to fall for the aura, not the substance. It isn't until they get older that they realize the value of character."

Trevor flashed Jenny a look of displeasure, which only intensified his resemblance to Shane. "*Character* is something my father sorely lacked, along with morals and decency."

Jenny wondered if this deep-rooted anger Trevor had toward young women had manifested itself into something horrible one June afternoon in 1988. Before she had the chance to elaborate on that thought, Kyle asked, "Did you happen to hear a phone message at your parents' house shortly before Stella was killed?"

"A message saying what?"

"I think you'd remember what it was about if you'd heard it."

"I don't think so, then," Trevor said. "Nothing stands out. Besides, even if I went to visit them, I wouldn't have played their messages. That would have been weird."

The notion made sense to Jenny.

"Can you tell me where you were the afternoon Stella was killed?" Kyle asked.

Trevor looked straight at Kyle. "I have absolutely no idea what I was doing the day Stella got killed. I mean, do *you* remember what *you* were doing on that day?"

"Nope," Kyle said flatly. "Sure don't."

Trevor let out a snort. "I hope this doesn't mean I'm actually a suspect in this thing. That would be ridiculous."

"Ridiculous or not, we're covering our bases," Kyle said as he closed his pad. "The fact of the matter is that your father's mistress ended up murdered. We would be remiss if we didn't investigate everyone who would have been upset by the affair."

"Well, you can investigate me all you want, but you'd be wasting your time. I assure you I didn't have anything to do with her murder."

"Okay, then, let me just ask you one more question. Where were you living at the time of the murder?"

"I lived in an apartment on Roseland Court."

Jenny recognized the name; those were the apartments that backed up to Stella's house.

Chapter 12

Jenny stood with Kyle in front of the series of buildings that comprised Roseland Apartments. "It's huge," she noted, recognizing how little justice the aerial view had done during her computer search. "I guess it's not surprising that both Colin and Trevor lived here."

"With its close proximity to Braynard College, I'm sure a lot of young people called this place home. It may have been *the* place to stay back then, or even now."

Jenny heard the faint sounds of the renovation coming through the trees, causing her to wonder how Zack had fared with his father. Sticking to the matter at hand, she added, "If the handprint on the back sill means the killer lived here, we may have a big suspect pool."

"Not necessarily. Stella must have been acquainted with her killer—she referred to him as *the son*. It could be Trevor, it could be Ed Pryzbyck, or it could be someone else who lived here and whose parent she knew."

Letting out a sigh of frustration, Jenny noted, "It's never easy. I wish there could just be one case where the killer is obvious."

"There was," Kyle said. "This one." He looked at Jenny out of the corner of his eye. "Nate Minnick was arrested within hours, remember? Cut and dry. Slam-dunk. See what it got them?" Patting her on the back he noted, "Any good investigator is going to look at multiple angles, even if one seems to stick out as the most promising."

Jenny furrowed her brow; she knew Kyle was right, but she still didn't like it. "Well," she said, "I guess we're not doing anybody any good just standing here; maybe we ought to call it a day."

"Actually, I'd like to take a look at Stella's old house considering how close we are to it. Maybe we could even walk there through the woods and get a feel for the path the killer took to get back here—if, in fact—that's what he did." He flashed a smile. "Investigate all angles, remember?"

Jenny had to laugh. "Yeah, we can take a walk. Oh...and I want to pay you. Every time I get home after seeing you I remember that I haven't paid you for your time yet." They started heading behind the apartment buildings toward the sound of the renovation. "Have you been logging your hours?"

"I have," Kyle admitted. "Does that make me a bad person?"

"No," Jenny replied, "it just makes you a man with a family to feed. So what's the damage?"

After pushing a few buttons on his phone, Kyle announced a number that most people would have found staggering. Jenny, on the other hand, simply asked, "Can I write you a check?"

Reaching the back of the buildings, the two started across the short patch of lawn that served as a buffer between the apartments and the trees. "You fascinate me, you know that?" Kyle remarked.

Jenny laughed. "Why, because I can cut a check for that amount?"

"In a word? Yes. Most people would be reaching for their credit cards right about now."

"Well, I've got to be honest with you." They reached the patch of trees and began their journey through. "Do you remember that first case where I asked you to track down Elanor Whitby for me?"

"I do," Kyle replied.

"Well, I wasn't exactly honest with you about why I wanted to find her."

"Jenny Watkins," he said with mocked offense as he cleared away some branches with his hands. "You *lied* to me?"

"First of all," she replied with similar feigned anger, "it's Jenny Larrabee. Watkins was the other husband."

"Oh," Kyle said sincerely. "Sorry."

"Don't worry; I forget too, sometimes." Jenny stepped in something mushy; she refused to look down and see what it was, choosing to believe it was only mud. "And second, I felt like I needed to lie. The reason I wanted to find her was because I moved into her old house and had gotten contacted by a spirit who encouraged me to find her. If I had come in claiming that, you would never have given me her address. You would have thought I was a lunatic."

"You know what?" Kyle said. "You're right. On both counts."

"I know I am; that's why I lied." They were nearing the end of the woods; Rob's house was becoming clearer. "Anyway," she continued, "I was able to solve a mystery for Miss Elanor just before she died, and she was so grateful that she left me the bulk of her estate…which my ex-husband took half of, but whatever. She left me the money under the pretense that I use it to help people, which is what I've been doing ever since."

"Your ex really got half?" Kyle asked. "That's a shame. That means you can do less good."

"I know, but I don't want to think about that," Jenny admitted as they entered Rob's backyard. She pointed to the slider that led to the deck. "See that? That's the door that had the bloody handprint."

"Mmm hmm," he said in affirmation. He looked behind them and declared, "It wouldn't have taken someone very long to run out the back and get into the cover of those trees."

"That's what I figured," Jenny said. They continued to walk around the side of Rob's house, eventually catching sight of the ever-present barrage of contractor vans that had been littering the driveway and cul-de-sac. "Wow," Kyle noted, "it looks like he's getting a little work done."

Jenny briefly summed up the story behind the renovation, but before she finished the tale, she noticed Rob outside talking to a man in Willy Sanders's driveway. She recognized that man to be the African American man from the pictures in Rob's hallway. Stopping in place to finish the explanation, she concluded by gesturing in the men's direction, "And on a different note, I think we might have our witness here."

"Most excellent," Kyle said. "Perhaps we should go introduce ourselves."

Jenny nodded. "That's what I'm thinking."

As Jenny and Kyle approached, she heard Rob say, "And here she is...my other guardian angel."

"I don't know about that," Jenny said with a smile. "How are you doing, Rob?"

"Great," he replied. "Just telling my neighbor, here, about all of the good work you're doing to my house."

Jenny extended her hand. "Hi, I'm Jenny Larrabee."

"Willy Sanders."

She glanced subtly in Kyle's direction, indicating that was indeed their witness. With a look that suggested he understood, Kyle shook Willy's hand as well, moving on to do the same to Rob.

It turned out Jenny didn't need to find a way to bring Nate Minnick into the conversation; Willy went ahead and did that for her. After a short discussion about the renovation, he added, "Rob tells me you're looking into the Stella Jorgenson case again."

"Yes, sir," Jenny replied. "I am under the distinct impression that Nate didn't actually do it."

"Are you sure about that?" Willy asked. "I saw that boy running out of the house all bloody with a knife in his hand."

"I know, but I think that was just an unfortunate coincidence. Let me ask you this, Mr. Sanders. Did you *hear* anything that day?"

He shook his head. "No, I was in my garage with the door closed, getting my lawnmower ready."

Willy spoke slowly, with an easygoing southern drawl that Jenny found remarkably relaxing. Jenny wondered if that had always been his way or if it had come with age.

He continued his story. "When I opened the garage door, I saw Nate running out of that house. I went over there to check on Megan and Stella, you know, to make sure everything was alright, and what I saw was horrible." Hanging his head, Willy clearly recalled the image that Jenny, too, had witnessed; she could understand why he was so disturbed by it.

With renewed energy he stood up straight and added, "I called 9-1-1 from their house, and the police and ambulances came a few minutes later."

"Was Stella still alive when you were there?"

He nodded solemnly. "Barely."

"Did she say anything to you?"

"She looked like she was trying to, but I was on the phone, and the cord only went so far. I couldn't get close enough to hear her. The 9-1-1 operator told me to stay on the phone until help arrived, so I did." He looked sad again. "When I look back on it, I wish I didn't. That way I could have potentially heard what she was trying to say. Those would have been her last words."

"If it makes you feel any better, I think I know what she was trying to say," Jenny replied.

Willy looked at her incredulously. "You do?"

Jenny nodded. "Her dying message was to *look for the son*."

Furrowing his brow, Willy repeated, "Look for the son?"

"She told that to Nate, so I know she wasn't referring to him when she said it." She squinted as she looked up at him. "Do you have any idea who she might have been talking about?"

"The son," Willy muttered again. After some deliberation, he added, "No, I'm afraid I don't."

At that point a car approached, changing the expression on Willy's face from confusion to delight.

"Is that them?" Rob asked.

"It sure is."

Before long, a young girl came running out of the back of the car. "Grampa!" she yelled as she approached Willy, her smile about as wide as it could get, displaying a distinct and precious lack of front teeth.

"There's my Rosie," Willy replied as she practically form tackled him with a hug. "How's my baby girl doing today?"

"Good." She let go of her embrace and looked at her grandfather. "Can Brianna and Sarah have a sleepover tonight?"

Rob laughed out loud at the request. "That has to be a new record. I knew the question was coming, but it only took about ten seconds."

Willy placed his hand on the little girl's head. "It's okay with me if it's okay with Mr. Denton." He turned to Rob before adding, "The girls can sleep here tonight if you want...that'll give you and Amber a little break."

Rob raised his eyebrows. "I just might take you up on that."

A smiling woman approached, followed by a lanky boy who appeared to be in his early teens. He had cornrows in his hair and a faint moustache, his hands stuffed deeply into his pockets. He looked at the ground and shuffled his disproportionately large feet as he walked. As with many kids his age, awkward had apparently opened its mouth and swallowed this boy whole.

Willy addressed the woman. "Hey, Sherry," he said with a hug. "How are you doing?"

"Good, Dad. How are you?"

"Can't complain."

She smirked at Rob as she released her father's embrace. "I hear the girls are already conjuring up a sleepover."

"Of course," he replied. "Tonight would probably be the best night to have it, because we're actually going to head out of town soon." He explained the renovation to Sherry, adding that it would be easier for everyone involved if the family wasn't home. "We're going to visit my sister in Savannah for the weekend."

"Well, at least the girls get to have a little bit of time together before you leave," Sherry said pleasantly. "I know Rose has been looking forward to seeing them for weeks."

Willy turned to the lanky young teen. "What's the matter, Shawn? You too cool to say hi to your ol' Grampa these days?"

A smirk appeared on Shawn's face, revealing a mouth full of braces, but he didn't say anything.

"Okay, I get it," Willy said. "You don't have to hug me. But you do need to give me a handshake. A *real* handshake. None of that chest-bump thing you kids do these days."

Shawn shook his grandfather's hand goofily.

"My goodness, he's getting tall," Rob noted.

Sherry's eyes widened. "You are not kidding. He's grown six inches in the past year. This year I am literally buying his school clothes on the last day of summer; any sooner than that and I'll be sending him off to school in high-waters."

Willy turned to both of the kids and said, "Okay, now you two go on in there and give your grandmother a hug. She made cookies for you." He patted his grandson on the shoulder. "That means you too, Shawn. You're never too old or too cool to hug your grandmother, you got that?"

Another goofy grin signaled that Shawn had found the comment amusing, but he didn't want to admit it. Rose eagerly bounded into the house with Shawn shuffling his heavy feet behind her.

Focusing his attention on his daughter, Willy spoke once the kids were out of earshot. "It's starting to look like Nate didn't kill Stella Jorgenson."

Sherry's face reflected dismay. "What?"

He gestured toward Kyle and Jenny. "That's why they're here...they've re-opened the case."

Looking as if she were contemplating the implications, she took a step backward. "So Nate went to jail when he didn't do this? And the Minnicks had to sell their house?" She looked at her father. "And the person who did this has been out on the street all this time?"

"I know," Willy agreed. "It's so scary to think that the guy could have come back and gone after one of you kids."

Jenny's phone rang, so she looked at who was calling; her eyes grew wide when she saw the name. Glancing at Kyle she announced, "It's Charlie Patterson."

Kyle seemed confused. "Who?"

"Charlie Patterson," Jenny replied, "Megan's ex-husband. He was at the cookout."

After stepping away from the group to have her conversation with Charlie, Jenny returned with a smile. Kyle eyed her suspiciously, asking, "Okay, what did he have to say?"

"Well, it appears we can cross one Mr. Ed Pryzbyck off the list of suspects," Jenny announced.

"Oh yeah?"

"Yup. Charlie said they were all at a movie while the murder took place...Rainman, to be precise. Charlie, Megan, Ed and Renee had gone to a matinee."

Kyle nodded as he absorbed the words. "So, I guess our focus is back on the Burke family?"

"It looks that way." Jenny smiled, exuding that all-too-familiar *I'm about to ask you a favor* look. "And along those lines, I'm wondering if there's someone you can find for me."

With her belly full from dinner, Jenny sat with Zack at the dining room table, once again looking through documents from the case. She rubbed her tired eyes. "This is exhausting. There is so much paperwork here."

"Indeed," Zack muttered.

Jenny reached over to the pile of papers, pulling a fresh one off the stack. As soon as she placed the page in front of her, she felt an undeniable wave of familiarity come over her. Looking at the document more closely, she noticed it was a hand-written letter on lined paper.

An image flashed in her mind. Stella lay on the floor covered in blood; the coffee table was overturned; papers stuck out from underneath it.

Papers.

"I think I might be on to something, Zack."

He set down the document he was reading. "Oh yeah? What's that?"

"It looks like a letter...to someone named Karen." She glanced up to look him in the eye. "It's only half done."

Seeming confused, Zack posed, "How did that get in there?"

"I think it was part of the crime scene," Jenny replied. "It looks like Stella may have been in the middle of writing this when the attack happened."

He scooted his chair a little bit closer to Jenny. "What does it say?"

Jenny scanned the letter. "The beginning is just your typical stuff," she disclosed. "Asking how this 'Karen' is doing, congratulating her on her raise at work...but then it gets interesting."

Zack didn't respond; he simply raised his eyes to look at her.

"It says here, *I screwed up. Last weekend I accidentally invited Shane and Colin to the same cookout. I don't know what I was thinking. I was able to keep things civil, but it wasn't easy. It took a little creativity on my part.*

"*After that night, I decided this whole thing was getting out of control. I think Colin is in love with me, and Shane has been getting a little too possessive. He has started to act like he doesn't want me to talk to any of the guys at work...he never came out and said that, but I can sense it. I told him on Thursday that I think we should cool it for a while. He didn't seem too happy about that, but I don't know how upset he can really be. The man is married, after all. I just hope he doesn't make life too difficult for me at work. I should have known better than to get involved with a co-worker.*

"*I plan to have a similar talk with Colin this weekend.*" Jenny looked at Zack. "And that's where it ends."

"I thought you told me that Doctor Burke had broken up with Stella."

"That's what he'd claimed," Jenny confirmed, "but when I spoke to Ed Pryzbyck, he said that Stella had been the one who was getting tired of Doctor Burke." She looked back down at the letter in her hand. "It looks like Ed's version of events is a little more accurate."

"I think that's petty damning," Zack noted. "Stella broke up with Doctor Burke, she ends up dead, and then the good doctor claims that *he's* the one who initiated the break up? It sounds to me like he might be trying to cover something up."

Jenny tapped her finger to her chin. "You know, all this time I thought maybe Trevor had done this, and he had been acting on behalf of his mother." She looked up at Zack. "Is it possible Trevor did this because he was acting on behalf of his *father?*" Before Zack had the chance to respond, she answered the question or herself. "But Trevor hated his father, or so it seemed. Why would he have committed murder to avenge him?"

"Is it possible Trevor committed the murder for himself and *not* for either of his parents? Maybe he personally had something against her."

Jenny's eyes widened as she pointed at Zack. "You know what? He did. He said he despised her and every woman like her, meaning women who fell for Shane's lines and obvious BS. He insinuated that they were too stupid to recognize a man who was genuine."

"Like him?" Zack raised an eyebrow in Jenny's direction.

Jenny was stunning herself with her own revelations. "Do you think maybe Trevor had a thing for Stella? Could that be what's going on?"

"Well, the way I see it, if he made a specific point to mention that girls couldn't recognize a genuine guy, I would imagine he was referring to himself." Zack shrugged his shoulders. "He may have had feelings for Stella, or he may have just been bitter in general."

"Oh my God," Jenny said with dismay. "This may be it. This may be the motive we've been looking for."

"Did Trevor say where he was the day of the murder?"

She shook her head. "He claimed to have no idea what he was doing that day."

"Maybe that's something you ought to look into."

"I imagine Kyle might be doing that already." She gave the notion some thought. "Although," she added, "I did task him with finding a Miss Danielle Church, one of Shane Burke's young mistresses. I want to get a feel for what it was like to date the good doctor, or at least what tactics he used to attract these women. In order for an older man to have so many younger mistresses, he must have had some tricks up his sleeve."

"Or big bills in his wallet."

Unwilling to make a conjecture on the matter, she simply said, "Maybe I should give Kyle a call. It may be more important for him to find out what Trevor was doing that day instead of tracking down Danielle Church."

Zack nodded. "Sounds like a good idea."

With the touch of a button she dialed Kyle, who had been put on her speed dial long ago.

"Hello, Mrs. Larrabee. Long time no see."

Jenny smiled. "I know; I'm pestering you a lot this week."

"No, you're not pestering me at all. In fact," he replied, "I was getting ready to call you. I've got a couple of pieces of information for you."

"Oh? Does one of those pieces happen to be Danielle Church's contact information?"

"Why, yes, it does, although her name is now Danielle Kraemer." Kyle proceeded to give her Danielle's address and phone number.

"Did you ever know that you're my hero, Mr. Buchanan?"

Kyle let out a laugh. "You might want to wait a minute before you say that. I haven't disclosed my second discovery yet."

"Uh-oh. Does this mean I'm not going to like it?"

"I'm pretty sure you won't. You remember that incredibly nice neighbor, Willy Sanders? The one who witnessed Nate Minnick running from the house?"

"Yes." Jenny felt her blood beginning to run cold.

"Well, it turns out Mr. Sanders has a son."

Chapter 13

"You're right," Jenny said as she hung her head. "I don't like that news."

"I knew you wouldn't—but we've got to investigate all angles, remember?"

She sighed with defeat. "What made you look into that?"

"Well, I remember Willy saying something about *you kids* running around the backyard with a killer on the loose. That's what started me thinking. I guestimated Sherry's age to be in her late thirties, which would have put her in her early teens in 1988. It wasn't unreasonable to think that she might have had an older brother, and it turns out she did...in addition to three younger siblings."

"How old was the older brother when the murder happened?"

"Seventeen."

"Seventeen," Jenny repeated with dismay. "Don't you think that's a little young to commit such a brutal murder?"

"Yes, but we can't ignore the fact that Stella's last words were to look for the son."

Indeed they had been. Although, Jenny had to admit that she hated this idea; the Sanders family had seemed like such a nice group of people. The last thing she wanted to do was bring Nate's loved ones some peace, only to turn around and strip it away from Willy's family. She much preferred the idea of the killer being one of the Burkes.

"Well, I had a different idea about what she meant," Jenny said, hoping she was going to turn out to be right. "I was thinking she'd been referring to Trevor Burke, but maybe his motive had been more self-serving than I had anticipated before. He said he didn't like Stella or any woman like her...maybe his anger and hatred got the best of him."

"It could be," Kyle said. "I'm certainly not suggesting we zero in on Marcus Sanders. I am just trying to prevent us from getting tunnel vision with the Burkes."

Jenny nodded slightly. "I can respect that. I have developed—and zeroed in on—theories in the past that have turned out to be wrong."

"We all have," Kyle replied, "which is why you keep looking at different suspects until the proof against one becomes irrefutable."

"Okay then, can you look into Marcus Sanders a little bit while I talk to Danielle Kraemer? I'm hoping I can get ahold of her tomorrow."

"That sounds like a plan," Kyle said. "And for the record," he added, "I'm also hoping this investigation into Marcus Sanders turns out to be a bust."

Jenny was grateful to get under the covers. She turned to Zack, who had already gotten into bed, and asked, "How did things go with your father after I left?"

"About like you'd expect," Zack said. "He walked around undermining everything I did."

"You know something?" Jenny began. "I think if you just approach things a little differently, you might be able to tolerate your dad a little better."

"And how, exactly, should I be approaching things?"

"Well, I've only known Andy for a few days, but there are some things that I have already learned about him...like, for instance, he will *always* be critical of the choices you make. As soon as he asked you what material you planned to use on the handicapped ramp, I knew he was going to come up with a reason why it was a bad choice, no matter what you said. Honestly, honey, there was no way you could have answered that question correctly."

"Okay, if you're trying to get me to like my father better, it isn't working."

Jenny laughed. "You haven't let me finish. What I'm suggesting is that you stop trying to win his approval. You'll never get it. And that's *his* hang-up, not yours. If you just learn to expect the criticism, it won't be so frustrating when it comes."

"See, what gets me, though, is that he only directs that kind of criticism toward me. If my brother Tim was building the ramp, there would have been no way he could have answered the question *wrong.* He could have told my father he planned to make the ramp out of dog shit, and my dad would have been like, *Oh, dog shit. That's great! What a creative use of natural resources. Maybe I'll make my next ramp out of dog shit, too.*"

Jenny found herself giggling again, although she said, "He would not have said that."

"You want to make a bet?"

Acknowledging that Zack had been largely correct about his father's behavior in other respects, she simply said, "Well, for whatever reason, your father has decided to make you the victim of his constant nit-picking. If you say black, your father will inevitably say white. If you can come to terms with that, you may not take it personally when it happens."

At that moment Jenny felt a flutter in her stomach. She paused for a second, lying frozen, wondering if she had just felt the baby move for the first time.

Unaware of what she'd experienced, Zack replied, "It's hard not to take it personally when I'm the only person he directs it to."

The flutter returned. "Zack," Jenny said with muted excitement, "put your hand right here." She guided his hand to the spot on her belly where she'd felt the sensation.

"Did the baby move?" Zack asked.

"I'm not sure. I think so," she replied. "Just give it a minute."

After what seemed like an eternity, she experienced the tapping sensation again. "Did you feel that?"

"Yeah, I did," Zack said with a huge smile. "It's little Steve, knocking on the door to get out."

Jenny looked down at her belly and poked it with her finger. "No big ideas, baby. You've got a few more months before you get to come out."

"He's eager to start playing some football," Zack noted.

"I don't know," Jenny said. "It felt more like she was practicing her tap-dance routine to me." She leaned up on one elbow. "And speaking of our daughter, I thought of a girl's name in the car today."

Zack held up his hand. "I don't know why you would focus on such foolishness, but continue."

"What do you think of the name Ashley?"

Zack remained quiet for a moment. Finally he muttered, "Ashley Larrabee. That does have a nice ring to it. Too bad it will never happen…unless, of course, one of our sons marries a woman with that name."

Flopping back down on the bed, Jenny playfully muttered, "You are such a butthead."

"I am merely being realistic."

"So, do you like the name Ashley or not?"

"You know what? I do. I think we should go with it…as our plan B, of course."

"Of course." Jenny couldn't help but smile. She had really liked the name when she'd thought of it, and she was glad that Zack agreed. At that moment she felt another flutter. "Oh—there she goes again. It appears our little Ashley is quite a dancer."

"Wow," Danielle Kraemer said on the phone. "Nothing like having the biggest regret of your life come back to haunt you."

Jenny let out a small laugh. "I know. I'm sorry to do this to you, and I assure you I'm not judging you. It's just that one of Shane Burke's young mistresses ended up dead back in 1988, and I figured contacting you would be my best shot at figuring out what life was like for her while she dated him."

"Is he a suspect in her murder?" Danielle asked with surprise.

"Not officially," Jenny replied. "I'm just trying to find out everything I can about some of the people in her life. Do you mind if I ask you a few questions?"

"No, go right ahead," she said. "Although, for the record, I'm not proud of what I did."

"Believe me, there is a long list of things that I did when I was younger that would go under the umbrella of *regrettable*." Jenny was specifically thinking about her relationship with her ex-husband, Greg. "We all have things we're not proud of...unfortunately yours has become important in a murder investigation, so it needs to be discussed." Jenny referred to the notepad containing the list of questions she had made in advance. "I guess the first thing I'd like to know is how you and Shane met."

Danielle let out a small snort. "How we met is indicative of our whole relationship. I was working at a department store at the mall—I was maybe, what, twenty or twenty-one at the time? I was in college. Anyway, he came in and said he was looking for a gift for someone special, and he needed some advice about what to get. I walked around the store with him for quite a while, trying to help him decide on the perfect gift. We chatted, and I had to admit he was quite charming. He eventually decided on a pair of diamond earrings and went on his way. I didn't think anything of it, but he came in a few days later and asked for my advice again. He didn't buy anything this time, but he said I'd been so helpful the time before that he wanted my opinion again. He asked if a woman would prefer flowers or chocolates; I laughed and said *both*. We talked some more, and he asked what kind of music I liked. I told him I was a *huge* Beatles fan.

"Well, wouldn't you know...the next time I went into work, all of the girls were giggling and calling me over to the service desk. You can probably guess what was waiting there for me...earrings, chocolates, roses, and every Beatles tape ever made...along with a little card that apologized for coming on too strong, but stating that I had taken his breath away when he saw me." She changed her tone to reflect her displeasure. "Now how is a naïve twenty-year-old girl supposed to react to something like that?"

"Wow," Jenny said, "I guess he really did pull out all the stops."

"He did, and at that age I wasn't equipped to handle it."

"What did you do?"

"Well, he came in to the store a day or two later, asking me how I liked the presents. I wasn't sure what to say. He was quite a bit older than me and wearing a wedding ring, so I just said that I liked the gifts and I thanked him."

"How did you end up dating?"

"In my defense, he addressed the wedding ring right then and there. He told me that he and his wife had conceived a baby when they were teenagers, and he married her. However, he also told me she was schizophrenic, and the signs of her mental illness didn't start coming out until after the wedding. He said at that point she had pretty much lost all touch with reality, but he didn't have the heart to leave her. He needed to take care of her and provide her with a home. However, he also said he was lonely and looking for the companionship she couldn't provide."

Jenny marveled at just how low Shane had stooped to get a young woman by his side. The disgust she had previously felt for him had grown exponentially. "And you were young enough to believe that," Jenny said with compassion in her voice.

"I was, unfortunately, although now I realize it was just a horrible lie," Danielle said. "But at the time, I figured that if he was just looking to go out and cheat on his wife, he would have simply removed the wedding ring. I didn't think he would have made up such an elaborate—and awful—story when he could have just told me he was single."

"That's reasonable logic," Jenny said. "Speaking from experience, I usually trust what people have to say. I think that's the curse of the honest person…if you generally speak the truth yourself, you assume others do the same."

"Exactly. And at that point in my life I hadn't learned that some people are just liars. What sickens me is that I actually ended up feeling sorry for the guy. That's why I agreed to go to dinner with him that first night; I thought maybe he needed a shoulder to cry on."

"Okay, I'd like to interject something here," Jenny said definitively. "You should absolutely not beat yourself up over the affair you ended up having with Doctor Burke. He was a grown man taking full advantage of the kindness of an inexperienced young woman."

"I know," Danielle said. "I've tried to convince myself of that, and on some levels I have forgiven myself, but it's still hard. Believe me, I am painfully aware that I am now the older wife who has lost some of her appeal. I often think about how much it would hurt me if my husband cheated on me with some perky little college student, and yet I did that to Shane's wife. I was her worst nightmare come true."

"If it makes you feel any better, you were one of many. Even if you had turned him away, his wife still would have been in the same position. Besides, if there's one thing I've learned, it's that you can't beat yourself up for the decisions you made when you were younger."

"Thanks," Danielle replied; Jenny could tell the gratitude was genuine. "'Unfortunately, I've spent a good deal of time doing just that. Sometimes I question how I could have been stupid enough to fall for his lies, but then I realize where I was at that point in my life. Honestly, I was a pretty easy target. If you consider they type of guys I was used to dating before Shane came along—college guys—it makes sense that I was so receptive to his advances. For the years leading up to Shane, the only dates I went on consisted of walking to keg parties, watching the guy drink way too much and then warding off his sloppy sexual advances at the end of the night. But when Shane presented me with the flowers and the earrings and that *card*...I felt like the most important woman in the world. I had never been treated at that level before, and I guess it was very appealing to me."

"It would be to any woman that age," Jenny said. "Actually, it *was*. Like I said, his tactics worked on a lot of young women."

"He was a master," Danielle noted, "that's for sure."

"How long did you two date?"

"It's hard to say. We went out platonically for a while before anything turned physical. At first we just talked a lot...let me tell you, he knew exactly what to say, too. There he was, this older, established doctor, asking me all kinds of questions about my life like I was the most interesting person in the world. And when I talked, he *listened*. I always had his full attention. So, even though I was a little skeptical about his intentions at first, after a while I actually came to accept that his feelings for me were genuine...that I wasn't just some young conquest for him. It was at that point that I allowed things to become romantic between us. I guess that was about six weeks in, maybe?" Her tone once again changed to reflect her irritation. "And wouldn't you know, after a few rolls in the hay, he dropped me like a ton of bricks."

Jenny hung her head, unable to mask her disgust for this man. "Oh my God, I'm so sorry that happened to you."

"Ah, well, live and learn, I suppose," Danielle remarked. "Although, I will say that was quite a blow to my self-esteem at the time. After dealing with nothing but college guys who seemed to all want the same thing, I thought that maybe this older man actually saw some value in me. I believed that a mature guy would have had his priorities straight and would have liked my intelligence or my sense of humor...but just when I let my guard down and allowed myself to start to fall for him, he disappeared, like all of the twenty-year-olds I was used to. I became very pessimistic after that, thinking that my dating life was *never* going to get better. It seemed like the older guys were also only after one thing. It was a very depressing time in my life."

If Shane had been in front of Jenny at that moment, she would have punched him in the eye. "Well, I see you eventually did go on to get married, so your romantic life had a happy ending after all."

"Oh, yes, it did. It turned out that Shane was the exception, not the rule. Most guys did straighten out their priorities as they got older. But now that I'm an adult and I look back on the situation, I wonder what was wrong with him. It isn't normal for a married man in his thirties to feel the need to prey on young women like that. He must have had a serious complex or something."

Jenny laughed out loud. "To say the least."

She concluded her phone call with Danielle, thanking her for her honesty and insight. After the conversation was over, Jenny looked over her notes, trying to see how Shane's selfish behavior could have translated into a potentially fatal relationship with Stella.

"He dropped Danielle when she started to fall for him," Jenny muttered to herself as a light bulb went off in her head. "And that was something Stella never did." That could have explained why his relationship with Stella had lasted longer than all of the others. She may have been a tougher nut to crack. Unlike all of Shane's other, short-lived mistresses,

Stella had a take-him-or-leave-him attitude, which he may have actually found irresistible. Megan had even mentioned that Stella had tried to break things off with Shane a few times, but he wouldn't have it. He poured on the charm in an attempt to keep her...probably so he could eventually be the one to break up with her once she rounded the corner and let her emotions become involved.

Asshole.

Jenny tapped her pen on the table as she considered this latest development. Then she froze as she realized something was missing from the crime scene...something that could have explained the trail of blood that led to the back door.

Jenny immediately headed into the dining room to look at the crime scene photos one more time.

As she approached the end of the cul-de-sac, Jenny noticed Andy's car among the contractor vans. "Oh, dear," she said out loud to herself. "Here we go again."

She got out of the car nonetheless and headed toward the house. The Denton family was packing up their van in the garage, apparently getting ready to visit Rob's sister in Savannah. She decided to approach them first. "You guys heading out?"

Rob looked up when Jenny spoke. "Oh, hey there. Yeah, we're taking off. I gave your husband the key; I figure it will be easier for them to do what they have to do without us in the way."

Jenny smiled. "It also might be nice to have a functioning bathroom for the next few days, which you apparently won't have if you stay here."

Rob's wife approached Jenny with a look on her face that spoke volumes. She appeared to be on the verge of tears. "I'm Amber Denton, Rob's wife. I can't tell you how incredibly grateful we are for everything you and your husband are doing for us. I mean, we don't even *know* you." A tear did eventually work its way to the surface. "Rob calls you and Zack our guardian angels, and I couldn't agree more."

"We're happy to help," Jenny said genuinely. "The person you should truly feel indebted to, though, is Elanor Whitby, the founder of *Choices* magazine; she left me most of the money in her estate with the instructions that I help people with it. All I'm doing is holding up my end of the bargain."

"Well, I can't thank all of you enough. It's truly amazing to see the kindness of strangers in action." She wiped her eyes. "It restores your faith in mankind, you know?"

Feeling overcome with emotion for this family who had endured so much, Jenny reached out and gave Amber a hug. "Truly, it's our pleasure. Now if you don't stop, you're going to get *me* crying."

Amber laughed and released the embrace. "Sorry—I guess I can't help it."

"Well, before I get too mushy, I'd like to go inside if you don't mind. Something occurred to me about the crime scene last night, and I want to go in and see if I can get another visual."

Amber nodded. "Go right ahead." She gestured toward the door that led from the garage to the house.

Jenny stepped inside and saw the beautiful new hardwood, as well as the guts of the master bathroom strewn about on a plastic sheet on the floor. Andy came out of the bedroom, stepping over some pipes and what used to be the bathroom sink. "Well, hello, Jenny."

"Hi, Andy. How are you doing?"

"Good. I figured I'd give Zack a hand today...you know, make sure he's doing it up right."

At that point, Zack also emerged from the bedroom wearing gloves and holding a crowbar. Behind his father, he raised the crowbar and made a gesture that indicated he wanted to club Andy over the head with it, causing Jenny to struggle not to laugh.

Seizing the opportunity to prove her point from the night before, Jenny looked up at Zack and asked, "What type of hardwood is this, honey? It looks nice."

"It's bamboo." He wiped the sweat from his forehead with the back of his glove. "It's more scratch-resistant than most hardwoods, so the wheelchair shouldn't bother it."

"You should have gone with Bolivian Cherry," Andy said. "It's even harder than bamboo...but I guess it's too late now."

Jenny widened her eyes and looked at Zack, silently saying, *See?* Zack simply shook his head.

"So, what brings you here?" Zack asked. "Well, first, come here and give your big daddy a hug." He approached Jenny with wide arms, his sweaty and dirty t-shirt clinging to him.

Jenny laughed and cowered. "It's not necessary. Really. You don't need..." She became engulfed in his sweaty arms as he rubbed his nasty body up against her. He released his embrace with a goofy giggle, and Jenny remained frozen in place. "Gee, thanks, honey." She wiped herself off with mock disgust.

"That was gross and uncalled for," Andy said. "Why would you do that to her?"

"It's called fun, Dad," Zack replied. "You should try it sometime."

"Anyway," Jenny said loudly before things got too ugly, "what brings me here is I want to take one more look at the crime scene. I'm working on a theory."

"Do you need us to leave so you can concentrate?" Zack asked. "We can go outside for a little bit if you want."

After some deliberation, Jenny said, "Do you mind? Construction noise isn't exactly conducive to getting a reading."

"Not at all." Zack turned to his father. "Come on, Dad. Maybe we can go out and have lunch."

"Isn't it a little early for lunch?" Andy posed.

"Okay, I'll eat lunch," Zack replied as he headed down the steps to the front door. "You can watch, since apparently you think that would be the more appropriate thing to do." The men walked outside.

Jenny shook her head once the guys were safely out the door; they certainly knew how to get on each other's nerves. Switching gears to focus on the matter at hand, she relaxed and walked toward the spot where Stella had once lay. She knelt on the ground, just as Nate had done, closing her eyes to get a vision of what the room had looked like twenty-five years earlier. After a moment, she was able to see Stella looking horrified on the ground with the overturned coffee table nearby. Jenny focused on the papers that stuck out from underneath—papers, but no pen.

She looked around, trying to ignore Stella's desperate and futile cries for help. Try as she might, she was unable to see any type of writing utensil. The vision faded, and Jenny was faced with the conclusion that an ordinary pen may have turned into a weapon on that fateful day, hopefully causing her killer to leave a trail of blood that would lead right to his doorstep decades later.

While Jenny sat contemplating her latest notion, Zack walked alone through the front door. "Where's Andy?" she asked.

"He left, thank God," Zack replied. "He got a call from one of his construction teams that there was a problem or something." He shook his head. "I don't know for sure what's going on, but I'm just glad he's gone."

"Well, I've got a little theory I'm working on," Jenny said with muted excitement. She explained her idea about the pen. "I'm thinking that blood the forensics team took did belong to our killer, who was suffering from what was hopefully a deep and painful puncture wound."

"That's gross but cool," Zack replied before guzzling some water.

"I wonder how long it will take to get the DNA results back on those stains."

"They implied it will take a while," Zack said. "Although, she's waited twenty-five years for justice. Hopefully a few more months won't be too painful for her."

"Stella isn't the one waiting for justice, remember? It's Nate we need to worry about."

"At least he's not sitting in jail while all of this is going on. That does alleviate the urgency a little bit."

Jenny looked at Zack, whose sweaty shirt had largely dried and whose messy hair had an element of sexiness to it. "You know, it turns me on when you use big words like that."

"It's the testosterone in your bloodstream, my dear Jenny," he replied with a pat on her shoulder. "You'll find that you get turned on when the wind blows."

She smiled and gave him a kiss that admittedly sent a little tingle of excitement through her body. Before she got carried away, she stepped back and retrieved her phone from her purse. "I'm going to make a couple of calls, I think. I have some questions that I'd like answered."

"I'm going to install a wall-mounted handicap shower chair." He flashed a smile as he headed back toward the bathroom. "Have fun."

She returned the smile. "You too."

Megan answered the phone after two rings. "Hi, Jenny. How are you?"

"I'm doing great," Jenny replied. "Thanks for asking."

"Are you making any progress on the case?"

Letting out a sigh, Jenny said, "It's hard to say. I'm making discoveries...only time will tell if it's actual progress."

"Well, I guess that's something."

"It's better than nothing," Jenny admitted. "Well, the reason I'm calling is because I am under the impression that Stella was in the middle of writing a letter when she was killed, and the letter was addressed to a woman named Karen. Do you happen to know who that was?"

"I sure do. Karen was Stella's sister in California. They used to write letters all the time...this was back when there were no cell phones and long-distance phone calls were too expensive. It was the best way for two people to keep in touch on a budget."

"So, I imagine they were close, then. Maybe Stella had disclosed something to her that might give us an idea about who was responsible for her death?"

"It's possible."

"Do you happen to know Karen's last name?"

"It was MacNamara at the time. I'm not sure if it still is."

Jenny jotted down the name on the back of a receipt from her purse. "Perfect. Thank you. One more thing...and this question may be a little strange. What type of pens did you ladies use in your house back then?"

"What type of *pens?*"

"Yes...did you use anything special?"

"Well, I can't say what we used on a regular basis, but Stella had a really nice fountain pen she had gotten for five years of service at the hospital. She used that whenever she wrote her sister." Her voice trailed off. "She was proud of that pen."

"A fountain pen?" Jenny asked. "I'm not sure I know enough about pens to know what a fountain pen is."

"It's one of those pens that has a metal..." she paused before saying, "*thingy* on it. It almost looks like a tip of a feather pen that the colonists would dip into ink."

Jenny understood the visual. "A very pointy metal tip is what you're saying."

"Exactly."

She felt her nerves surge. "Well, thank you very much for that information. It's actually very helpful."

"No problem. Let me know if you need anything else."

"Will do," Jenny said with a smile. "Will do."

Jenny took a seat on the Denton's couch, reflecting on her latest theory. A fountain pen certainly could have done a lot of damage, and there appeared to be no pen at the scene. Perhaps it had been lodged into her killer and he walked out the door with it. Zack's words entered her mind, and she repeated them softly. "Gross, but cool." Her train of thought was interrupted by her phone ringing. It was Kyle Buchanan. "Hello?"

"Jenny," he said with relative urgency. "Is there any chance you can come to my office?"

"Sure." Jenny was surprised by the request. "When do you need me?"

"If you could come now that'd be great," he replied. "I got a phone call that you won't believe."

Jenny stood up to head toward the door, pulling her keys out of her purse as she walked. "Who was it?"

"None other than Katherine Burke," Kyle said. "She's on her way to my office right now. She said she had some things she wanted to discuss."

Chapter 14

Jenny arrived at Kyle's office to find him already engaged in a conversation with Katherine Burke. She rapped gently on the door with one finger, and Kyle gestured with his hand for her to come in. Katherine turned around with a smile. "Hello, again."

Jenny extended her hand. "Hi, Mrs. Burke. Good to see you."

Katherine shook her hand and pleasantly said, "You as well."

Kyle looked incredulously at Jenny. "Mrs. Burke, here, was just telling me that there was a little more going on between Stella Jorgenson and her husband than just a working relationship."

Jenny's jaw dropped, but when she turned to Katherine, she saw a well-put-together older woman with her hands folded on her lap, sitting there casually as if she were talking about her favorite recipes. "She and my husband were sleeping together. At least, I assume they were."

Jenny made a failed attempt at responding, but all that came out was a little sound.

Katherine continued, "You can't possibly think I didn't know what was going on all those years."

"But if you knew…" Jenny said, looking back and forth between Katherine and Kyle. She didn't know how to finish her statement.

"Why didn't I leave?" Katherine asked with a knowing smile.

All Jenny could do was nod.

"For the same reason I married Shane in the first place...we had a child together."

"But..." Jenny stammered, "by the time Stella came around, Trevor was an adult."

"Yes, but I also had a life and a routine that I liked very much." Katherine repositioned herself in her chair. "Believe it or not, Shane and I co-existed quite peacefully. We were friends—very good friends. My life in that house was pleasant...it's just that when it came to getting our needs met romantically, we had to look elsewhere."

We? Jenny once again found herself unable to respond.

Fortunately, Kyle kept his composure. "So, can I assume that means you had your share of extra-marital affairs as well?"

The well-coiffed woman turned to Kyle. "No, I only had one, but it lasted for fourteen years."

Feeling weak in the knees, Jenny sat down.

"He was a business associate of mine," Katherine continued. "His name was Clint Havershack."

Believing the answer to her question was about to be a *no*, Jenny asked, "Does Shane know about him?"

Katherine shook her head. "I don't believe so. Shane was so concerned with himself that he never paid enough attention to me to catch on." She rolled her eyes. "He thought he was so slick...getting away with all of these affairs without me knowing. Meanwhile, I was aware of every bit of it. *He* was the one who had no idea what was going on."

Jenny was still stunned. "How did you know about his affairs?"

"Do you have any idea how many scorned women called the house to tell me what my husband was doing behind my back? It seems Shane infuriated a new woman every few months."

"And that didn't bother you?" Jenny replied with shock.

Katherine turned to Jenny and plainly said, "My relationship with my husband was nothing more than friendship. We hadn't been romantically involved, if you will, in years. Quite honestly, I was very much in love with Clint at the time. I really wasn't all that concerned with what Shane was doing...or who he was doing it with."

Jenny shook her head rapidly, trying to make sense of what she was hearing. "But...if you were in love with Clint, why didn't you leave Shane and begin a life with him?"

"Clint wasn't the type of man you settled down with," she explained. "He was very much married to his job. And he lived in Pennsylvania; we saw each other when I traveled there, but I had no desire to move. Like I said, I liked my life. Besides, I was happy just having a long distance relationship with him. I know this may be difficult to understand, but I liked the excitement I got to feel during those business trips to Philadelphia. In fourteen years, my relationship with Clint never got stale. If he and I had settled down together, there's no doubt I would have eventually grown tired of him—just like I had done with Shane."

While the notion logically made sense, in a way, Jenny was still flabbergasted. Somehow Katherine looked much too elegant to be speaking these words.

Kyle, on the other hand, seemed less interested in the logistics of the Burke's free-wheeling lifestyle. "Mrs. Burke, you say that you received a lot of phone calls from angry young women...did you ever happen to get a phone message from an angry young *man?*"

She smiled knowingly, turning her gaze to Kyle. "Yes...and that's exactly what I wanted to talk to you about. Although, from the sound of it, you may already know about it."

"Why don't you tell me what you wanted to say, and I'll see if it aligns with what I know."

Katherine began with a sigh. "Just a few days before Stella was murdered, we received a phone message from an angry young man who claimed that Shane had been sexually harassing Stella at the workplace...forcing her to date him in order for her to keep her job." Katherine made a face and shook her head. "Now, I knew that wasn't true. Shane valued his job far too much to do anything that foolish. He would have never jeopardized his career. Besides, he had no shortage of women who were willing to go out with him. He wouldn't have needed to coerce anyone into a physical relationship."

She continued, changing her expression to be more serious. "My concern is that young man may have become angry at Stella if he realized she was lying about the nature of her relationship with Shane." She lowered her eyes. "I hadn't said anything about this until now because I've been operating under the assumption that the neighbor had done it. There was no need to bring it up. But now that I know the case has been reopened, I felt like I needed to come tell you what I know...I just didn't want to talk about it in front of Shane when you came to the house. When I found a business card you left for him, I decided to get in touch with you."

"Well, thank you for that," Kyle said. "We were aware of the phone call already, but we do appreciate your honesty." He casually flipped the page in his notebook and asked, "While we have you here, would you mind answering some questions about Shane's relationship with Trevor?"

"With Trevor?" Katherine asked, looking surprised. "I guess I can." She seemed like she didn't know why that would be necessary.

"Excellent," Kyle replied. "Did Trevor and Shane have a good relationship?"

Katherine looked down and shook her head. "I'm afraid not."

"What was the source of the problems between them?" Kyle asked.

"Truthfully?" Katherine said as she sat back in her chair and crossed her legs. "Trevor's existence."

Jenny looked at Kyle with just her eyes.

Katherine continued, "I think he always resented Trevor because he had been an accident. We were teenagers when we conceived him, and Shane felt pressure to marry me. Honestly, I believe there's a part of Shane that thinks I got pregnant on purpose." She looked at Kyle with wide eyes. "I assure you, I did *not* do it on purpose. What seventeen-year-old gets pregnant by design?"

"I don't know of any," Kyle said flatly. Jenny admired his ability to appease whoever was speaking to him.

"I actually think that's part of the reason Shane felt the need to date so many younger women; he felt like I trapped him. He never got to sow his wild oats, so to speak. And then when I fell in love with Clint and became detached, I guess that was the final straw."

"*You* checked out of the marriage first?" Jenny asked.

Katherine nodded, for the first time looking a little sad." It wasn't much of a marriage anyway. Like I said, we were really good friends."

Thankfully, Kyle was able to remain more focused. "So, tell me, specifically, what Trevor and Shane's relationship looked like."

"It didn't look like anything, and that's the problem," Katherine said. "At first, when Shane was going to college and then to medical school, he claimed he was too busy studying to have much time for Trevor. I'm not sure Trevor noticed at the time because we lived in my parents' basement, and his grandparents spoiled him to death. But once Shane got a successful career and we moved out on our own, I think Trevor started to realize how little his father was involved in his life. Whenever Trev wanted to spend time with Shane, he was always just handed a toy and told to go play. I think Shane believed that was good enough...that Trevor was just looking for entertainment, and Shane had just provided it—by handing him a toy that was purchased with the money Shane had earned while working long hours at the hospital. But Trevor was looking for a relationship with his father, and I'm afraid he didn't get that.

"Now, I don't want to make it sound like Trevor had an awful childhood," Katherine added. "We lived in a great neighborhood—once again provided by Shane's hard work—and he was surrounded by friends. He played a lot of sports. The one element that was missing, though, was a bond with his father."

Jenny leaned forward onto her elbows. "How was Trevor around women? Was he charming like his father?"

Katherine shook her head. "No. In fact, he was just the opposite of his father. While Shane could sweet-talk with the best of them, Trevor had a difficult time even striking up a conversation with a woman. I was worried about him, actually. I didn't think he'd ever get a girlfriend or settle down."

"Did he, though?" Jenny asked.

"Eventually. He was in his early thirties, though, before he met Valerie. She was a good fit for him—her first husband had been a jerk, so she was able to appreciate Trevor's kindness." Pride exuded from Katherine's eyes. "He may not have been smooth, but he was always kind."

Always kind, Jenny thought. Not according to her latest theory.

Katherine continued. "Do you mind if I ask why there's this interest in Trevor? I figured you'd be more concerned with that young man who called my answering machine."

"Just covering all our bases, ma'am," Kyle said.

Katherine looked remarkably unconcerned. "You can't possibly believe this involves Trevor at all. That would be ludicrous. He didn't even know Stella Jorgenson."

Kyle looked up at Katherine with a smile. "Then I guess you have nothing to worry about."

Once Katherine had left the office, Kyle and Jenny were able to speak more freely. "*That* was crazy," Jenny said almost immediately after the door closed. "Here I was spending all this time feeling sorry for Katherine Burke…I never in a million years suspected that the infidelity was mutual."

Kyle let out a laugh. "From the sound of things, she started it. The way she described it, Shane started fooling around only *after* Katherine began her affair with Clint."

"I'm completely floored," Jenny admitted.

"That's because you are new at this," Kyle said. "You wouldn't believe some of the things I've seen in my career as a private investigator. This is actually on the tame side."

She shook her head. "I don't even want to know."

Looking square at her, Kyle replied, "You really don't."

Disturbed, Jenny was anxious to change the subject. "Okay, so let's talk about Trevor, shall we? He was apparently socially awkward around women," Jenny noted. "Isn't that often a common characteristic of the serial killer?"

Kyle raised one half of his mouth into a smile. "Yes, it is. But first of all, we're not dealing with a serial killer. Stella alone seemed to have been a target. And second, I believe it's more of the rectangle/square thing. Serial killers are usually socially stunted somehow, but not every awkward guy murders women."

Jenny giggled. "Well, it was worth a shot."

Kyle flipped to a different page in his notebook. "I got some information about Marcus Sanders earlier today. It's what I was looking into when I got the call from Katherine."

"Good news, I hope?" Jenny said. "Something that says that there's no way Marcus could have done this?"

"Nothing that good, I'm afraid," Kyle admitted. "His record is clean as a whistle, though. No arrests...not even any parking tickets. Served as a Marine for a while, then came back and went to school." He scanned his notes and concluded, "Nothing here that indicates he would be a prime suspect."

"Good," Jenny said.

"Well, not so fast," he remarked. "There's nothing here that says we should focus on him, but I also couldn't find anything that would allow us to cross him off our list, either. I think I may need to talk to Willy again to see if Marcus had any kind of relationship with Stella, or if it's possible that she only knew him well enough to refer to him as *the son*."

Jenny laughed at her own misconception. "When you said *relationship,* at first I thought you meant something romantic. That would have been rather upsetting considering she was twenty-six and he was seventeen."

"I didn't mean that, but it wouldn't have been the strangest thing I've ever seen."

Holding up her hand, Jenny remarked, "I don't want to know." With a smile she added, "Although, there is something I *do* want to know. I'd love it if you could tell me the whereabouts of Stella's sister. It sounds like they were close, and Stella may have had some conversations with her that she didn't have with Megan. Perhaps the sister can give us some insight about whether or not Stella's romantic life could have led to her death."

"I think I can arrange that," Kyle said. "What's her name, do you know?"

"Well, in 1988 it was Karen MacNamara. I'm not sure if it still is."

Kyle started to type into his computer. "I guess we can find out."

Jenny hid out in the confines of the guest bedroom at the Larrabee's house. She looked at the phone in her hand, reluctant to dial, unwilling to tell this unsuspecting woman that her sister's killer was not the man she'd thought it was for the past two and a half decades. Time ticked by with Jenny fully aware that each passing second was one more second of peace Karen MacNamara got to enjoy. For that reason, Jenny held on to the phone for a little while longer.

Eventually, she did dial, and a woman picked up on the other end. "Hi, my name is Jenny Larrabee. I'm looking for Karen MacNamara."

"This is."

"Hello, Karen. I'm very sorry to have to make this phone call, but I have been conducting an investigation in Mumford Springs, Georgia, looking into your sister's murder from 1988."

Despite Jenny's pause, Karen remained silent on the other end of the line. Jenny knew this couldn't have been easy to hear.

"Unfortunately, I am under the impression that the original investigators were a little hasty in their conviction of Nate Minnick. It turns out he had a very low IQ, and there's a good chance his confession had been coerced."

"But there was other evidence against him," Karen noted. "It wasn't just the confession that got him convicted."

Jenny described the misconception surrounding Nate's quick departure from Stella's house. She also mentioned the blood trail to the back door and the unexplained handprint on the sill of the slider. "I genuinely hate doing this to you, but I would like to ask you some questions about what was going on in Stella's life at the time of the murder. I'm hoping to gain some insight on who may have had the motive to do something like this."

"My God," Karen whispered. "I thought this was over."

"I know," Jenny said apologetically, wanting to soften the blow a little bit. "Why don't you start by telling me a little bit about Stella during her happier times?" Jenny was sincere when she added, "I always like to get to know the people I seek justice for—it motivates me to find their killers."

Karen began with a sigh. "Oh, Stella. She was a few years younger than me, and she was the typical younger sibling. You know how they say most presidents were oldest children, and most Hollywood actors and actresses are the youngest? Well, that was certainly true for Stella and me."

Karen continued, "I was always jealous of her ability to work a room. Even when she was little, she always managed to attract attention to herself. Don't get me wrong; she didn't make a *spectacle* of herself or anything—she just had a way about her that made people want to be around her."

Jenny knew those types of girls; she had never been one of them. "I assume you are a little more on the quiet side?" Jenny posed.

"Very much so. But strangely, Stella and I got along just fine. We were yin and yang, you know? We provided each other with balance."

"How many years apart were you?" Jenny asked.

"Three," Karen replied, "which seemed like it was a big difference until we got older. Once we were both in high school, we started to actually become friends, and we remained that way until the end."

"Her roommate told me you two wrote letters all the time."

"All the time."

Jenny smiled; being close had nothing to do with proximity. These sisters were apparently as close as sisters could be from opposite sides of the country. "So, how did Stella come to be married so young? Honestly, I was quite surprised to hear she had been widowed at age twenty-four."

"You and me both. It was such a shock. We grew up in Michigan, where you can imagine that winter sports are quite popular. Stella had always been a figure skater; she was quite good, actually. She could skate from the time she could walk. When she was in high school, she met Pete Jorgenson at the rink—he was a hockey player, and his practices were at the same time as Stella's. They hit it off right away, and they got married when she was fresh out of college."

Jenny thought back to her own situation and how miserable she'd been after marrying her boyfriend from college. "Were they happy?"

"They seemed to be," Karen replied. "They laughed a lot. Pete was a very funny guy. And they had a lot going for them—he was a couple of years older than Stella, so he was already established when they got married. They were able to get a house right away, and their lives seemed perfect. That was, of course, until the day Pete never came home from work."

Jenny hung her head. "That must have been positively awful for Stella."

"It was," Karen replied. "To make matters worse, they had just started trying to have a baby. She went from thinking she was going to have a family with Pete to not even having Pete. It was an incredibly tough time for her."

"I can imagine."

"The final kick in the pants was that he didn't have life insurance—I guess at twenty-six he didn't think he needed it. So, not only did she lose her husband and the baby she never got to have, she lost her house, too."

This was getting sadder by the minute. "I guess that's when she moved in with Megan?"

"Yes," Karen replied. "That was the one thing that worked out nicely in all of this. Megan's uncle had just moved out of that house, but he didn't want to sell it. He rented it to Megan and Stella for a very cheap rate." Karen paused before adding, "I suppose you wondered how two single women got to be in a three bedroom house in an established neighborhood."

Jenny had never wondered that, but now she realized she should have. Feigning competence, Jenny noted, "Well, now it makes sense."

"Unfortunately, that's where things spiraled out of control for her."

"So I've heard," Jenny replied sympathetically.

"Well, at first it wasn't that way. I went months without hearing from Stella. I would write, but the letters always went unanswered. I would call, and Megan would tell me that Stella was there but didn't want to come to the phone. She was just about as depressed as anybody could be. Then it was like a switch flicked or something…suddenly she went from depressed to manic. I would get letters from her often, and they were always filled with details about her latest sexual escapades and how this one has a crush on her or that one wants to ask her out. It was just plain crazy."

"I guess that's not the Stella you knew."

"Not at all. I mean, she was always social, but this was different. She was being *self-destructive*." Karen's tone became solemn. "It was difficult to witness from three-thousand miles away. There was only so much I could do to help her. I tried to convince her to go to counseling, but she said there was no need. I wish I'd pushed it harder. She might still be alive today if I did."

Ah, guilt, Jenny thought, *the common thread among those left behind.* "The way I see it, there's one person and one person only who is responsible for Stella's death, and I intend to find out who that is."

Karen's tone reflected her disappointment. "I was under the impression we already knew who that was. Although, something about him did surprise me…"

"What is that?" Jenny asked.

"Well, Stella had told me that one of her teenage neighbors had a crush on her, so when I found out the eighteen-year-old next door had done it, I wasn't shocked. But when I saw a picture of him in the paper, I was confused."

"Why?"

"Because Nate Minnick was white," Karen noted, "and Stella had told me the teenager with a crush on her was black."

Jenny helped Ellen fix dinner while Zack looked online for handicapped rails for the Denton's bathroom. Jenny continued to marvel about her earlier meeting with Katherine. "It was amazing," she said. "There was this woman, just sitting there with a smile on her face, talking about how her husband had been repeatedly unfaithful to her with a multitude of younger women."

Ellen lowered her eyebrows. "That *is* very strange."

Zack looked up from his computer. "I don't think it's that weird."

Jenny regarded her husband with dismay. "Should I be frightened by that comment?"

"No," Zack assured her, "but you should be able to relate to it."

"Okay, you're going to have to elaborate on that a little bit."

Zack laughed. "You said she was in love with someone else, right?"

"Right."

"Well, imagine the scenario...suppose you and Greg had a child together, so while you didn't love him anymore, you didn't want to get a divorce, either. Now, here I come into this scenario, and you fall in love with me because...well...I'm totally awesome."

Jenny and Ellen looked at each other with unimpressed smirks on their faces.

Zack continued, "But because I'm this totally eligible, successful and unbelievably handsome bachelor, you knew I wouldn't marry you. So what do you do? You stay married to Greg to keep your family together, and you begin a decades-long affair with me."

"Clearly," Jenny said sarcastically.

"Well, whether you agree that it's the correct approach or not, hear me out," Zack reasoned. "If you did find yourself in that scenario, would you care if Greg was seeing someone else?"

Jenny had to admit he was right. "No, I guess I wouldn't."

"Exactly," Zack replied, "and neither did Katherine Burke."

Turning to Ellen, Jenny noted, "He does have a point."

"Yes," Ellen agreed, "and he has an obnoxious way of presenting it."

"What, because I described myself as unbelievably handsome? The truth hurts, mom.".

She shook her head and rolled her eyes. "Honestly."

"You know," Zack began, "I'm sure you'd be surprised just how many people have skeletons in their closets. People seem all normal and suburban, but when the truth comes out, sometimes it's shocking."

Jenny put her hand on her hip and said, "You know, I will say that when I called the Pryzbycks, a man answered the phone. I assumed it was Ed, but when I asked for Ed, the man said Ed wasn't home. I then asked for Renee, and she came to the phone. I wonder who that man was...maybe they're one of those couples with a skeleton."

"See?" Zack said. "You never know."

Jenny laughed as she grabbed the plates to set the table. Turning to Ellen, she asked, "Will Andy be home in time to eat with us?"

"I don't think so," Ellen replied. "Something came up at a jobsite today, and he told me he had a lot going on. That's not unusual, though."

She headed back toward the oven and put on a mitt. "When you're married to a guy who runs a company, you don't really ever have a set schedule."

"Speaking of *that guy*," Zack said, "he's been a regular presence at the Denton's house lately. What on earth possessed you to tell him I was there?"

Ellen shrugged. "I just thought it would be nice if you two could work together. I figured it might help you get along better." She opened the oven door and reached inside.

"Trust me; it's not helpful."

"Well, I had to do something," Ellen said. "I've had just about enough of your constant bickering."

"Unfortunately, putting us together on the same jobsite is not the answer. Maybe you can install a glass partition in the house and keep us apart. That might work."

Ellen sighed with frustration.

"You've got to admit," Jenny began, turning to Zack, "it's been nice of your father to let us stay here all this time. We were only supposed to visit for a couple of days, and it's turned into something a lot longer. He's opened his home to you, even after the rift you two had." She nudged Zack with her elbow. "*And* he's been letting you use his car so you and I can be in two places at once."

"Yes," Zack admitted, "I suppose that is nice."

A tug began to resonate within Jenny; she glanced up and saw Ellen putting out the dinner she had worked so hard to prepare, but Jenny knew she needed to find out what the pull was about. "Sorry," she said flatly, slipping into her trance-like state. "I've got to go." She began to head toward the front door.

Jenny heard Zack briefly explain the situation to his mother before he scurried out the door behind her. They climbed into her car and drove in silence as Jenny allowed the tug to lead her. Before long, they pulled up in front of the Denton's house, where a familiar car sat in the driveway.

"Great," Zack whispered softly enough to allow Jenny to remain focused. "My father is here."

Still feeling a strong tug, Jenny got out of the car and walked briskly toward the front door. When she approached, she noticed the glass door was closed but the wooden door was open. Peering through, she saw the reason she was supposed to be there.

"Oh my God, Dad!" Zack yelled.

Jenny reached into her purse to call 9-1-1.

Chapter 15

Zack rushed through the door to find his father lying on the foyer floor, dazed, looking blankly toward the ceiling. "Dad, are you okay?" he demanded as he knelt by Andy's side.

"I fell," Andy said slowly. His voice was barely audible.

Jenny heard the voice of the 9-1-1 operator in her ear asking for the nature of the emergency. Jenny stated the Denton's address and asked for an ambulance. "My father-in-law fell down the steps," she added quickly. "He has blood coming from his ears and nose."

"Is he conscious?"

"Yes."

"Okay, make sure he doesn't move." The operator told Jenny how to position her hands under Andy's neck to stabilize him; Jenny did as she was told. "Now, keep him still until the paramedics get there. Help is on the way."

Andy moaned, causing Jenny to close her eyes and wish she was anywhere but there.

"So, you just *fell*?" Zack asked.

Andy managed to mutter, "Blacked out."

Zack looked around. "What are you doing here by yourself, anyway?"

He responded with only a moan.

Zack stood up and paced nervously in the small confines of the foyer as he called his mother, mumbling something about the contractors leaving the door unlocked while he dialed. Although Jenny couldn't make out Ellen's words, she could hear the urgency in her voice through the phone. Zack instructed her that they would probably be going to Saint Mary's hospital, which was closest in proximity to Rob's house.

In the meantime, the 9-1-1 operator was asking a lot of questions about Andy—questions that Jenny couldn't answer. She had to serve as the go-between as the operator inquired about Andy's age and health history. She felt horrible making Andy answer so many questions when he was in such obvious pain.

After what seemed like an eternity, sirens became audible, signaling that help was on the way. Jenny dropped her head in relief, eager to relinquish her neck-stabilizing duty to the professionals. The paramedics soon entered the front door, squatting down next to Andy. Organized chaos took over as Jenny stepped back out of the way and the ambulance workers wrapped Andy's neck with a horrible-looking contraption, clearly designed to keep him still. They placed him onto a stretcher and eventually carried him out to the ambulance to be taken away. Zack confirmed that they would be bringing him to Saint Mary's hospital, and he and Jenny jumped into her car, following the ambulance out of the cul-de-sac.

Time seemed to stand still in the waiting room. Ellen had joined Zack and Jenny, as had Zack's brother, Tim, and his wife, Hannah. Had the circumstances been more pleasant, Jenny would most likely have marveled at the physical resemblance between Zack and Tim, despite the fact that their personalities couldn't have been any more different.

Ellen looked positively green with worry, sitting with her arms folded and her legs crossed, her foot bobbing rapidly with nervous energy. Zack's expression looked markedly different, reflecting regret and shame in addition to apprehension. Jenny imagined he was reliving the day's interactions with his father, remembering every argumentative word that was said, most likely wishing he could suck them all back in.

Eventually Zack spoke, breaking the painful silence that had blanketed the family. "Do you think Nate led you to the house because my father was hurt?"

Jenny nodded slightly. "I can think of no other reason I'd get pulled there. Once we discovered your father, the tug stopped."

Zack absorbed the words. His tone was soft when he replied, "I guess we owe him one, then, don't we?"

Jenny looked at her feet. "I'm working on that."

A doctor came out from between two double-doors. "Larrabee?" he asked.

Ellen was the first to stand up. "That's us."

"Are you his wife?"

"Yes," she said nervously. "How is he doing?"

"He's stable. His vitals are good. He's got a slight skull fracture, but it's a simple fracture—meaning it's just a crack in the bone with no displacement or depression. We expect that to heal without the need for surgery. He also has a concussion, which will keep him bedridden for a while, but that, too, should eventually get better on its own. Our larger concern, actually, is what caused the fall to begin with. He claims he got incredibly dizzy when he went up the stairs, and then he woke up on the floor. When he recovers from these immediate injuries, the next step in the process will be to find out if he has some kind of heart issue that led to the fainting spell."

Relief washed over the entire family. Ellen placed her hand on her heart. "Thank you so much. Can we go see him now?" Ellen asked.

"He's being transported to a room where he will be admitted," the doctor explained. "Once he gets settled, you can pay him a visit."

The family thanked the doctor again and gathered their things, waiting for word that they could say hello to Andy.

Everyone stood around Andy's bed except for Ellen, who sat by his side holding his hand. Zack's facial expression had returned to normal once he'd learned that his father was going to be okay, and his sense of humor had apparently also made a resurgence as well. "Dad," he said jokingly.

"You could have messed up the floor with that big ole hard head of yours. We just put it in, too. It's too soon for it to get all dented."

Andy didn't smile, and his response was weak. "The floor won that battle, don't you worry about that."

Jenny glanced up to look at Zack, who smiled in a way that showed deep down he really did love his father. "Now aren't you glad we went with bamboo instead of Bolivian cherry? Wood that hard could have killed you."

Closing his eyes, Andy softly replied, "You should have used rubber."

"Actually, *you* should have used the chairlift. That would have solved this whole problem, you know."

Jenny saw Andy's lip curl into a slight smile, although Ellen swatted at Zack with her hand. "Will you leave him alone? He's been through enough already. He doesn't need you hounding him."

"I'm just messing with him, Mom. After what he put us through today, he totally deserves that."

The smile disappeared from Andy's face. "I need to talk to you." He pointed his finger in Zack's direction. "Alone."

Jenny lifted her eyes to look at her husband, whose face reflected the same surprise that she felt.

Zack's eyes scanned the room. "Now?"

"Yes," Andy replied weakly. "Now."

Ellen also looked surprised. "You want us to leave?"

Andy raised a finger toward Jenny. "Everyone except her. She stays."

Jenny had liked it better when she thought she was going to be excluded from their talk. Now nerves surged through her as she wondered what she was about to witness.

"I don't know about this," Ellen said apprehensively. "You two aren't going to kill each other while we're gone, are you?"

"I couldn't kill a fly right now," Andy muttered.

Ignoring his comment, Ellen looked at Jenny. "Do you promise to make sure things stay civil between these two clowns?"

Jenny made a face. "I'll do my best."

Ellen kissed Andy very gently before she, Tim and Hannah walked out into the hallway. Zack took a couple of steps forward and stood where Ellen had just been. He looked nervous as he asked, "What is it, Dad?"

Jenny shared in his uneasiness.

Andy swallowed; speaking seemed to be a struggle for him. "I was there for a long time, you know. I'm not sure exactly how long, but it felt like forever."

"Well," Zack explained, "it took us about a half an hour to get there from the time Jenny first got the feeling that something was wrong."

"Is that what happened?" Andy whispered. "That's why you came back?"

"Yeah, and it's a good thing, too," Zack added. "If Jenny wasn't a psychic, you could have been there all night."

Andy laughed as much as his weakened condition would allow. "Believe me, I thought I *was* going to be there all night." His eyes grew solemn. "I thought I was going to die there."

"Nah," Zack replied, keeping levity in his voice. "You're too hard-headed for that...both literally and figuratively."

This time Andy didn't look amused. "I deserve that."

Jenny stood frozen, glancing back and forth between father and son with just her eyes, afraid to move a muscle.

"You know," Andy continued slowly, "I spent a lot of time thinking while I was lying there...thinking about what I was doing there in the first place. I was there to check up on you. I was there to find mistakes in what you'd been doing. I've been doing it for days." He cleared his throat and swallowed, clearly finding the words difficult to say. "You're renovating a house to make life easier for a handicapped man for God's sake, and I went there to find flaws in your work."

Zack remained silent, wearing an expression unlike any Jenny had ever seen on him before.

"And you know what? I couldn't find any. Nothing you did wrong, anyway, so I picked on the choices you made." He slowly raised his hand, complete with the IV, and gently rubbed his forehead with a wince. "I'm hard on you. I know that I am, but it's because I worry about you." He let out a snort. "You were always fucking things up as a kid." Holding up a hand in Jenny's direction, he added, "Excuse me."

Jenny held up her hands in return, silently letting him know she hadn't been offended.

Andy continued, "You constantly joked around at the construction site. You were always late for work. I thought you'd never get anything right."

Jenny expected a wise remark from Zack about this being a lousy apology, but it never came.

"I guess I thought I had to watch every move you made to be sure you didn't mess up too badly...but you know what? That's not my job anymore." He pointed at Jenny. "That's her job now."

Jenny managed a smile.

"And as I lay there, thinking I just might die...my biggest regret was the way you and I fight all the time. I don't want things to be like that anymore."

Finally, Zack smiled. "Are you delirious, Dad?"

Andy closed his eyes. "Funny. You're a funny kid."

"Aren't I, though?"

"You're a wise-ass, that's what you are."

"But I'm a *likable* wise-ass."

Andy's expression reflected defeat. "Yes, you are. You're a likeable wise-ass. And you know what? You haven't turned out half bad." He pointed at Jenny again. "I think this one's been a good influence on you."

"She has," Zack replied. "And I think quitting the construction business has helped, honestly. I'm sorry, Dad, I really am...but building houses just wasn't my thing. It's not a reflection on how I feel about you...I just didn't like the job."

Andy didn't reply, but his face reflected understanding.

"Actually, you know what I didn't like about the job?" Zack continued without contempt in his voice. "I didn't like *who* we were building the houses for. Dad, those houses were frickin huge...way too big for any family to actually need that much space. And when I was in the design center, I can't tell you how many times people came in over and over again to change the shade of the cabinets, or go back and forth about whether they wanted chair rails or not. I just couldn't help but think those people had too much time and too much money on their hands...and both of those things could have been much better spent on something else.

"But, honestly, I'm actually having fun renovating Rob's house," Zack added with a guilty expression. "But that's because I'm doing it for a good reason...for a deserving person. I'm actually doing something I care about now." He lowered his eyes. "I'm sorry I couldn't have cared more about Larrabee Homes, but I just didn't."

Andy looked as if he was growing tired. "If you're going to devote your life to helping people, I can't fault you for that." His eyes closed into a long blink. "In fact, I'm proud of you."

Zack smiled. "Okay, now I know you're delirious."

Andy's eyes closed and remained that way. "But you're still a wise-ass."

Jenny turned on her phone as soon as she got back into her car in the hospital parking lot. She immediately noticed a missed call from Rob Denton and a voicemail to match. After listening to the message, she turned to Zack and said, "Rob is worried about what happened at his house. I guess Willy called him and told him someone had been carted off in an ambulance."

"You might want to give him a call back and let him know everything's okay."

"Yeah, I'll do that. He must be worried." Jenny dialed his number before turning the key to her car. He answered as she pulled out of her space.

"Hello?"

"Hi, Rob, it's Jenny Larrabee."

"Jenny...is everything okay? I heard an ambulance came to the house."

"Yeah, everything's okay," she replied. "Zack's father just had a dizzy spell and passed out on the stairs. He landed on the floor in the foyer and got a concussion and a slight skull fracture."

"Holy shit," Rob said. "Is he going to be okay?"

"The doctor seemed to think so. Apparently the bigger concern is what caused the fainting spell to begin with."

"Wow," Rob added. "Well, I guess if they can run some tests and figure out what the problem is, this little episode will be a blessing in disguise. It may ultimately save his life."

Jenny adored how Rob always looked at the positive side of things.

"So, were you there when it happened?" Rob added. "That must have been scary to watch."

"Actually, the scary part was that no one was there when it happened. He was stuck on the floor in the foyer for about half an hour, we think."

"I guess he's lucky you came by."

"Actually, luck had very little to do with it," Jenny noted. "I was led there."

"You were *led* there?"

"Yes, I'm assuming by Nate Minnick. I was at Zack's parents' house, when all of the sudden I felt the pull that told me I needed to go somewhere. The tug led me straight to your house, where we found Andy on the floor."

Rob remained silent on the other end of the phone; Jenny wondered if somehow she had upset him. After the silence became long enough, she asked, "Is everything alright?"

Rob cleared his throat, indicating that he had indeed been choked up. "Nate led you to my house that first day, too, didn't he?"

"Yes, he did." Jenny was unsure what he was getting at.

"You know," Rob began, "I've always said that I've had a guardian angel. I'm telling you, there's no reason I should have survived that car accident five years ago. I'll have to show you pictures of the car when I get back—it was nothing but a mangled piece of wreckage. Even the paramedics marveled at how I was able to live through that.

"But now that I know Nate was looking out for your father-in-law..." Rob sounded as if he was trying to maintain his composure. "Maybe it's not unreasonable to assume he was looking out for me that day, too."

Jenny couldn't help but smile. "It's possible."

He let out a deep sigh. "All this time I believed that kid was a murderer, and it seems like he's exactly the opposite. He's been *saving* lives."

Jenny loved the thought of that—if Nate could stop being regarded as a villain and instead be considered a hero, that would have definitely allowed his soul to rest in peace. "I agree with you," Jenny replied.

"We've got to clear that kid's name," Rob said with conviction. "Is there anything I can do to help with that?"

As much as Jenny didn't want to admit it, she replied, "Actually, there is. When I get back to Zack's parents' house and get access to my notepad, is it okay if I call you to ask you a few questions?"

"Sure," Rob replied. "What about?"

Jenny was reluctant to say the words, although she knew they had to come out.

"Marcus Sanders."

Chapter 16

"Marcus did tell me he once saw someone die," Rob said over the phone. "Actually, he said he didn't see them die, but he saw some injuries occur that ultimately ended up being fatal."

Jenny's heart sank at the prospect that Marcus had been talking about Stella.

Rob continued, "One day he and I sat down and had a few beers, and he opened up about his days over in Iraq. He was part of Operation Desert Storm and Desert Shield. He generally didn't like to talk about that time in his life, but that night the alcohol made him a little more chatty."

"What did he say about it?" Jenny asked.

"He told me that one of his buddies had stepped on a landmine. He described it as the most awful thing he'd ever seen. The kid lost a leg immediately, right there on the battlefield. Marcus said the screams can still haunt him if he lets them. Anyway, they were able to send the wounded soldier away to get help, but apparently he bled to death before he could get the proper treatment."

Jenny closed her eyes and hung her head; this was the type of story she absolutely hated to hear. However, she knew she needed to remain focused and remember the reason she was calling. "How did he react to it? I mean, did he say what kind of impact that has had on his ability to function?"

Rob seemed to consider the question. "He mentioned something about being able to compartmentalize it. He can put it away—tuck it safely back into the recesses of his mind. He did say that some things triggered the memory, alcohol being one of them. He also said he couldn't watch war movies, and firecrackers have a bad effect on him. But for the most part he is able to function on a daily basis, keeping that horrible memory repressed. He told me that knowing that it wasn't his fault has helped him tremendously...if he had felt responsible for it in any way he wouldn't have been able to sleep at night."

That last statement resonated with Jenny, but she was unsure what to make of it. Had he been speaking from experience? Or did he just make some innocent comment? Jenny hoped it was the latter.

Her conversation didn't result in any more insight, so she concluded the call and focused on her next task—talking to Megan to see if Stella had struck any type of friendship with the Sanders family or if they had lived merely as strangers next door. She dialed the phone, which rang several times before Megan picked up.

Jenny explained her reason for calling; Megan's response sounded sincere. "Unfortunately, now is not a good time. But listen...tomorrow I'm going to the Pryzbyck's for a cookout. Why don't you come? I'll have plenty of time to talk to you then. Besides, they said they wanted to meet you—they find it fascinating that you are a psychic."

"I wouldn't want to intrude," Jenny said.

"Oh, don't be silly. I'm planning to get there around three. Are you available then? You and your husband are both welcome to join us."

Jenny smiled. "Yes, I can be there then."

"Great." Megan gave her the address. "Oh—and bring a bathing suit. It's supposed to be hot tomorrow, and they have a pool."

"I didn't bring a bathing suit with me to Georgia," Jenny confessed.

"You can borrow one of mine, if you'd like."

"That's okay," Jenny said, trying to imagine her pregnant self in someone else's bathing suit. "I'll figure something out. I guess I'll see you tomorrow around three, then?"

"Perfect."

Jenny hung up and decided she should go check on Zack and Ellen, who were most likely still shaken from the evening's events. When she entered the kitchen, Ellen was trying to wrap up some of the dinner that had been left out when she'd quickly taken off for the hospital, and Zack was working on what appeared to be his second beer. Jenny started to help Ellen with the leftovers, asking, "Actually, do you mind if I heat some of this up before we put it all away? Ashley's getting hungry."

Ellen flashed Jenny a genuine smile. "Ashley, huh? Is that the name you've decided on?"

"It's only plan B, mom," Zack interjected. "It'll never happen. The kid's name is Steve all the way."

Jenny shrugged and placed her hand on her belly. "Well, either way, this baby is about to get cranky if I don't eat soon."

"Help yourself," Ellen said, lifting the lid of the container she'd just closed. "In all of the excitement, I'd forgotten you hadn't eaten."

"I'm surprised Zack hasn't reminded you," Jenny said with a smile. "He's usually all about the food."

He held up his beer. "Still working on the appetizer at this point." He glanced at Jenny. "So, did you learn anything about Marcus?"

Jenny reiterated what she'd heard from Rob. "I don't know what to make of it, honestly. I'm going to visit with Megan tomorrow to see what type of relationship they'd had with Marcus, and maybe pick her brain to see if there is anyone else who should be put on the suspect list." Jenny scooped some food onto a plate before turning back to Zack. "Do you want to come with me?"

Zack shook his head. "Nah. I'll let you do the honors. I want to take advantage of Rob's weekend away and get a lot done on his house. If I do take a break, I'll probably go visit my father."

"Fair enough. I just hope I can find some kind of evidence tomorrow that shows Marcus didn't do it. I won't feel very good about this if it turns out to be him."

"Well, justice needs to be served either way," Zack noted.

Jenny let out a sigh. "I just prefer when my bad guys aren't from such likable families."

Jenny wanted to accomplish two things before going to the Pryzbyck's cookout: she planned to stop by her old house and pick up something valuable that she'd left behind in the divorce, and she needed to get a bathing suit. Neither of these tasks seemed very fun.

After a leisurely breakfast, Jenny climbed into her car and headed to the house she had once shared with her ex-husband. Her mind began to wander as she drove, and she found herself wondering how much progress he had made on the renovation since she'd been gone. The once-beautiful house had been in terrible shape when they'd bought it, but Greg's intent had been to fully restore it.

Greg. Not her favorite person. Not by a long shot. She hoped to be able to avoid him when she went into the backyard and retrieved the aviary urn that had once housed Elanor Whitby and Steve O'dell's remains. She had originally hung the birdhouse near a cute flower bed by the edge of the property, believing that would have made Elanor and Steve happy. This was the house where they had met, after all, and they'd probably spent time together in that very spot.

When Jenny moved out, she deliberately left the birdhouse behind, thinking that's what Elanor and Steve would have wanted. However, since that time she'd come to regret that decision. She wanted the birdhouse in *her* yard, not Greg's, and she had since decided that Elanor would have wanted that, too.

She pulled up to the house, noting that the exterior looked the same as it had when she moved out. That wasn't surprising, though, considering Greg had mostly been focused on renovating the inside first. With a quick exhale, Jenny parked her car on the far side of the street and turned the key. She admittedly felt nervous, hoping she could sneak in the back, get the urn-turned-bird-house, and leave without detection. Although, if any birds were calling it home, she would have had no choice but to let it stay. She sincerely hoped that wasn't the case.

After tip-toeing through the front yard, she rounded the corner to the back of the house—where she didn't see the birdhouse hanging by the flower bed. She looked around, wondering if she'd actually put it somewhere else and just forgot, but she didn't see it anywhere. "What the hell?" she muttered as she expanded her search to include more of the backyard. Eventually, her eyes drifted to a pile of junk stacked up near the house with the birdhouse sitting on the ground in front of it.

"Are you kidding me?" Jenny demanded as she rushed toward the urn, whose bottom half was covered in a layer of dirt. She picked it up and immediately began to brush it off, cursing her ex-husband under her breath. He was such an asshole. Birdhouse in hand, she turned around to head back to her car, only to find Greg standing there, looking at her with an expression of distinct displeasure.

"Just what the hell do you think you're doing?" he asked.

"What the hell am *I* doing? What the hell were *you* doing when you put this urn with all of this junk?"

"It's a birdhouse," he said. "And it's junk."

"It is *not* just a birdhouse, and it's absolutely not junk. This once housed Elanor Whitby's remains...you know, that woman whose fortune you've been spending on yourself."

"Okay, first of all I didn't know that. And second of all, just what makes you think you can come onto *my* property and snoop around without permission?"

Contempt rose within her, reminiscent of vomit. She swallowed it down before saying, "Will you get off your high horse please? I just want this urn—which is obviously of no value to you anyway—and I didn't want to bother you." The truth was that Jenny didn't want to *see* him, but unfortunately that ship had already sailed.

"You didn't answer my question," Greg replied arrogantly. "In the future, if you're going to come here, I'd like you to ask for my permission first. Cindy might be here, and your presence might make her uncomfortable."

"How about this," Jenny said angrily. "How about I just never come back?"

"Even better," Greg said. "I really see no reason for you to be here anymore anyway."

The fact that she once loved this man was mindboggling to her. "Excellent. We're in agreement, then." With the urn firmly in her grasp, she walked around Greg and headed back to her car.

She still felt overwhelmed with anger as she started to drive away. At first the animosity was directed at her arrogant ex-husband, but then—as always—she turned the lens on herself. Why did she always let him get to her like that? She knew how he was. Why was she always surprised and irritated by the way he acted? Shouldn't she have just expected that type of interaction by now?

"Stop letting him bother you," Jenny said to herself as she drove in the direction of the store. "If he gets to you this much, he wins."

If only she could heed her own advice.

Jenny stood in the changing room with her two favorite bathing suits from the rack...one maternity, one not. Considering she was only four months pregnant and just starting to show, she decided to go with the regular suit first. After putting on the one-piece bathing suit, she looked in the mirror and crinkled her nose. "Oh dear," she said out loud. Things were worse than she had thought.

Her belly didn't look pregnant; it just looked big. Her hips had widened as well. She spun around to get a look at her rear end in the mirror and once again spoke out loud, "Holy mother of God." She hadn't looked at that part of her body in a long time, and apparently there'd been a lot of changes going on. While she'd always battled cellulite, now it seemed to have taken over the entire back half of her body. She had no idea she'd looked this bad. She hung her head when she considered that Zack had been looking at her all along, and he was fully aware of just how far things had come. She desperately hoped this was a symptom of pregnancy and would subside after she gave birth in November.

"Okay, then, the maternity suit." She realized she would most likely look like a lunatic to anyone else in the changing room when she emerged from the stall alone after having engaged in a full conversation with herself. Fortunately, she didn't care. She held up the black suit that looked more like an A-line little-black-dress and hoped that the skirt would successfully cover the cellulite explosion that had apparently taken place without her knowledge. Once the suit was on and positioned correctly, she took another look in the mirror. This image was not all that pleasant, either.

There was way too much fabric—enough cloth to cover a woman who was due last week, but Jenny had little more than a tiny bump. She grabbed the edges of the skirt and pulled them outward—her arms could practically reach full extension. She looked like Dracula.

Depression began to sink in. After the exchange she'd had with Greg earlier, this bathing suit debacle was just adding insult to injury. She hoped the afternoon with Megan wouldn't result in the realization that Marcus Sanders was a likely culprit, thus completing the bad day tri-fecta. That would have been too much to bear.

Returning to the matter at hand, she decided it was better to look like a vampire than it was to stuff herself into a suit she had no business wearing. Although, the thought did occur to her that maybe she just shouldn't swim.

As Jenny pulled into the driveway of the Pryzbyck's house, she noticed the neighborhood seemed to be family-oriented; it looked like a great place to live. She got out of her car and heard laughter coming from the backyard, causing her to head through the gate of the fence instead of to the front door. Once she rounded the corner, she caught Megan's eye.

"Oh, hey! I'm glad you could make it," Megan called. A couple that Jenny assumed to be the Pryzbycks turned her way and greeted her with a smile.

"Well, thanks for having me," Jenny said as she approached. Introductions were made, and Ed immediately offered her a beer. "I can't," Jenny explained. "I'm pregnant."

"I didn't know that," Megan said. "Congratulations!" An entire conversation about pregnancy and parenthood ensued. Jenny felt immediately comfortable around these people, under the impression that she could have remained friends with them if she had lived closer.

After Jenny was situated with a nice glass of ice water and a plate full of veggies and dip, the topic switched to her psychic ability. She told them about how she discovered her gift and that it turned out it was a genetic trait. For the first time, she was able to also say how it originated, having been told that by her grandmother just a couple of months before.

Megan and the Pryzbycks seemed mesmerized by her tale, which ended with a description of Nate Minnick's latest contact. In an attempt not to be too redundant, she left out the fine details, simply reiterating that she wanted to clear Nate's name by finding out who really killed Stella all those years ago.

"Which leads me to the reason for my visit," Jenny added. "I was wondering how much you could tell me about Marcus Sanders."

"Do you really think he's a suspect?" Megan asked.

"I wish I didn't," Jenny admitted, "but he is on my list."

"Well, he seemed like a nice enough kid," Megan said. "But then again, so did Nate."

"Were they friends? Marcus and Nate?" Jenny asked. "They were close to the same age."

"I never really saw them hang out together, but I also wasn't paying attention. I didn't realize it would ever matter." Megan thought about it some more. "I don't think they were enemies or anything...I just don't believe they were *friends*."

"How about Marcus and Stella? Did they ever talk at all?"

Megan shook her head. "I don't think they talked much, but I do think that Marcus may have had a little crush on her."

Jenny felt her blood run cold; perhaps Stella hadn't simply been manic when she'd made that observation. "What makes you think that?"

With a shrug, Megan replied, "He acted a little goofy around her. He would say hi if he saw her out there, but then he'd look down at the ground or stuff his hands in his pockets." Megan smiled. "He never had that reaction around me."

Renee chimed in. "He just had a thing for redheads, that's all. Don't take offense."

Megan laughed. "I didn't take offense. He was, what, sixteen? Seventeen? I wasn't exactly competing for his attention. Anyway, he would also make a point of hanging out in his backyard every time Stella went out to sunbathe. I noticed that, but I never said anything. I don't think Stella saw the connection, and I figured she might have been creeped out if she realized what was happening." She thought for a moment. "Not that Marcus was particularly creepy or anything...he was just young."

Stella *had* seen the connection, but according to Karen's account, she may have liked the attention. Although, Jenny had to admit this was the opposite of what she wanted to hear.

"Did you know Marcus at all?" Jenny asked. "Do you know what type of kid he was?"

"He seemed polite," Megan noted. "I think his parents made sure of that. He never said *yeah;* he always said *yes ma'am.* You know what I mean?"

Jenny smiled. "Yes, ma'am. I do."

Megan let out a little laugh. "Honestly, I never really saw anything that made me think twice about Marcus, or anyone in the Sanders family for that matter. They seemed like really nice people."

At that moment, a man walked around through the gate and into the backyard. He appeared to be in his forties with long hair pulled back into a ponytail, and he had several tattoos on his arms that extended up under the short sleeves of his shirt. Jenny heard Renee say softly, "What the hell is he doing home already? He's supposed to be looking for a job."

"Leo!" Ed called loudly. "You find a job?"

The man, who apparently went by Leo, shuffled his feet as he approached. "Nah," he grumbled. "Nobody's hiring." He came up the stairs and looked at Jenny with surprise. An expression of both confusion and pleasure graced his face. "Hey," he said. "And who have we here?"

"This is Jenny Larrabee," Renee said, her displeasure obvious. "And she's married, so no big ideas."

Leo held his hands up in a gesture of surrender. "You can't fault a man for trying, can you?" He spoke a little too slowly.

He proceeded to walk into the house, and as soon as Leo was out of earshot, Renee turned to Ed and proclaimed with disgust, "He's *high.* He's supposed to be out looking for a job, and he was out getting *high.*"

Ed shook his head. "I know."

"He's not holding up his end of the bargain, you know," she continued. "The deal was he could stay with us as long as he was trying to get his act together, but this isn't trying."

Suddenly Jenny knew who answered the phone when she had called before. This was apparently not a skeleton in Renee's closet, although she still wasn't sure where he fit into all of this.

She didn't have to wait long for an explanation. Renee turned to Jenny and said, "Leo is Ed's cousin. He'd fallen into some hard times, so we took him in...but there were some *conditions* to him living with us, and he's clearly not abiding by them...and honestly, I've just about had it."

"There's always one, isn't there?" Megan said with a smirk. "Every family has that one cousin that they wish they could deny being related to."

Jenny thought about Zack and the rest of the Larrabees as she dunked a carrot into her ranch dip. "I think I'm married to that cousin."

Megan laughed. "Well, he must not be that bad, then. I don't think anybody would marry my jackass cousin...he's just a horrible human being."

"That bad, huh?" Jenny asked.

"Oh, indeed," Megan assured her. "He has been in and out of jail, has had *restraining orders* put against him...he's a real *gem,* that one."

Renee scoffed. "It sounds like he would get along really well with Leo."

The wheels in Jenny's head started turning.

Renee turned to Ed and said, "Seriously, honey, I've had it with him. I know he's your family and all, but how much are we supposed to put up with? We're letting him stay here rent free, we're feeding him...and he's not putting any effort in at all."

"I know," Ed replied, clearly feeling torn between allegiance to his cousin and his wife.

Renee continued, "I'm not kidding, Ed. If this is how it's going to be, I want him out."

Leo stepped back onto the deck, invoking an awkward silence. There was a good chance he had just heard Renee's comment, although he wasn't reacting to it if he did. He merely took off his shirt and sat down on the edge of a lounge chair, taking a sip of one of the two beers he had brought out with him. He gestured the other toward Jenny. "You want one?"

"No, thanks," she replied. "I'm pregnant."

Leo shrugged. "Suit yourself." He placed the second beer on the deck next to him, looking quite satisfied with the prospect of keeping it for himself.

Jenny could feel Renee's animosity beginning to grow, so she took advantage of that moment to pursue her line of thinking. "Megan," she began, "you said your cousin had been in and out of jail. I also know your uncle owned the house that you and Stella rented together." She winced slightly to prepare herself as she added, "Did that particular cousin happen to be the son of the man who owned your house?"

Megan seemed confused. "Yes, he was."

"And how old is your cousin?" Jenny asked.

"Now? Let me think...I'm fifty-two, so he must be forty seven."

A little quick subtraction led Jenny to reply, "So he was in his early twenties back in 1988."

Megan's eyes got wide. "You're not suggesting..." She didn't finish the sentence. Clearly she was running through the scenario in her head.

"I'm not necessarily suggesting he did it," Jenny said. "I'm just looking at all angles. Did your cousin happen to live around you back then?"

Megan looked positively green. "He still lived with his father, so he moved out of the house I shared with Stella and into one about a half an hour from there."

"Would he have had a key to your house?" Jenny asked. "Or access to one?"

Megan placed her hand on her chest. "It's possible."

Leo leaned forward onto his elbows. "What's with all this talk about Stella?"

Jenny turned to look at him while Renee explained. "They've reopened the case. It seems the police may have gotten it wrong all those years ago."

Jenny's eyes drifted to the multitude of tattoos Leo had on his chest and arms.

"What makes them all of a sudden think that they were wrong?" Leo posed.

Jenny focused on one tattoo in particular.

"Well, that would be because of Jenny, here," Renee told him. "She's got some insight into the case that most people don't have."

The tattoo of the sun just under Leo's left collar bone had rays extending in every direction and a face that was distorted by a c-shaped scar that made the eyes and nose twist oddly. Jenny's blood froze in her veins as Stella's words echoed in her head.

Look for the sun.

Had she been interpreting the message wrong all this time? Had she been seeking out somebody's son when Stella had really meant that she should have been looking for a sun tattoo? And was that scar on the tattoo from the tip of the pen Stella had been using to write Karen when the attack happened?

But had Leo even been anywhere around Mumford Springs back in 1988? Or was this all just a very bizarre coincidence?

In a terrifying moment of sudden awareness, Jenny realized she had been staring. She slowly raised her gaze to Leo's face to see if she had been caught.

Apparently, she had been, and his expression only confirmed her suspicions.

She was looking into the face of pure evil.

His eyes were fixed on hers; a slight smile graced his lips. He seemed to be amused by Jenny's apparent realization, knowing that she was helpless to do anything about it at that moment. For a long few seconds, he continued to stare at her, sending a chill down her spine.

She made an involuntary sound that sounded like a cross between a gasp and a cough. "What's the matter?" Leo asked coolly as he reached behind him to grab his shirt. "Is something wrong?"

Jenny shook her head rapidly, looking down at her lap. "It's just the pregnancy." She placed her hand on her stomach. "I-I-I think these vegetables aren't agreeing with me."

"Well, be careful," Leo said in an ice cold tone, causing Jenny to raise her eyes to once again meet his. His smile grew slightly as he added, "You wouldn't want anything to happen to that baby, now would you?"

Jenny was so frightened she could hardly breathe. "No." Her shaky voice reflected her terror. "I sure wouldn't."

Renee's voice was mercifully sobering. "Can I get you something? Do you need more water or anything?"

Confused by the question at first, Jenny remembered that she had made a claim of an upset stomach. "Yes, please." She turned to Renee with a plastered-on smile. "More water would be great, thank you."

As Renee disappeared into the house, Megan called, "Bring me one too, please." Megan looked at Jenny. "I think I feel like you do right now. I'm horrified by the prospect that my cousin may have done this...but, you know, it wouldn't have been beyond him. Like I said, he's served jail time for assault and burglary. One of his girlfriends had a restraining order against him because he used to beat her." She placed her head in her hands and rubbed her eyes. "So, if it does turn out to be Thomas, how on earth are we going to prove it's him?"

Jenny chose her words carefully in an attempt to send Leo a message without tipping off the others. "Well, the forensics team took samples from a blood trail that went from the spot of the attack to the back door. There was also a palm print on the door sill that may have yielded prints." She cleared her throat. "If your cousin has a criminal record of any kind, and his DNA or prints are on file anywhere, it's only a matter of time before the police figure out it's him."

Leo shifted in his seat. Jenny pretended not to notice.

Renee returned with two glasses of water, handing one to each woman. Jenny accepted hers and drank eagerly, grunting with satisfaction. "Thanks. That really helped."

Megan didn't seem to feel much relief from the water. "I can't believe I never put two and two together," she declared. "Of course Thomas should have been a suspect."

"Don't blame yourself, Megan." Jenny felt like she was having an out of body experience as she spoke. "The police were so quick to arrest Nate Minnick...you would have had no reason to consider anyone else."

She shook her head. "But it shouldn't have sat right with me," she announced. "Nate was such a good kid; we never had any problems with him. He wouldn't have done something like that." She took another sip of her water. "It should have been obvious to me that the guy who did was some kind of chronic asshole with a history of violence toward women."

Jenny balled her hand into a tight fist as she silently pleaded for Megan to stop talking. She had no idea what Leo was capable of, and she had no desire to find out. "Well, we don't know for sure who it is yet. Right now all we can do is speculate." She looked down at her lap, hoping her words were having the desired effect of lessening any rage Leo might have been feeling. "I have learned in the past never to do that. You always have to let the evidence do the talking."

Leo spoke with his gaze fixed so intently on Jenny that she could feel it despite the fact that she continued to divert her eyes. "So, what makes you think it wasn't the guy they arrested?"

Jenny shrugged. "I just had a feeling." She swatted at a bug on her leg that wasn't there.

"She's a psychic," Renee said, her tone reflecting her continued awe. "Isn't that amazing?"

Leo leaned forward onto his elbow. "So, you know what's going to happen, then?"

What was that supposed to mean? Was that a threat? "No," Jenny said as she shook her head. "I don't see the future."

"She receives messages from the dead," Ed announced.

Jenny wished they would stop talking.

Once again, she felt Leo's ice-cold stare. "You know what it's like to be dead?"

Jenny cleared her throat again. "Yes and no."

Mercifully, Megan changed the subject. "Jenny, you really don't look well. Are you sure you're okay?"

Desperately wanting to get away from there, Jenny saw this as her opportunity. "Honestly, I'm really not feeling well at all," Jenny said. "I'm so sorry to cut this short, but I think it might be best if I get going."

"I understand," Renee said compassionately. "I'm sorry you're not feeling better."

Jenny simply nodded as she stood up, placing her hand on her stomach to feign discomfort. Reaching for her purse, she put the strap over her shoulder.

Leo stood up as well. "Let me walk you to your car."

The notion was horrifying. "Thank you for the offer, but that's not necessary," Jenny replied with an insincere smile. "I'll be fine."

"Well, do me a favor, then," Leo added. Jenny looked up at him as he expressionlessly warned, "Watch your step. I'd hate to see something bad happen to that baby."

Chapter 17

Jenny's heart was in her throat as she pulled away, looking in the rearview mirror the entire time to make sure Leo wasn't following her. She was utterly unsure what to do with her new information. Should she try to call Megan and warn her that she might be in danger? Or would that have only made things worse? Had leaving been the right thing to do in the first place? Or did she just jeopardize the safety of three people she had come to like?

She shook her head quickly, trying to calm herself. "Okay," she said out loud. "You're jumping the gun. You don't know for sure Leo did this. For all you know it could have been Marcus Sanders or Trevor Burke, or even Megan's cousin, Thomas." With another glance in the mirror for good measure, Jenny picked up her phone and dialed Kyle.

Fortunately, he answered, despite the fact that it was Saturday. "Kyle," she said instantly. "I need you to look into someone for me."

"You sound upset," he replied. "Is everything okay?"

"I don't know," Jenny said truthfully. "I honestly don't know."

"What does that mean?"

"I think I may have just stumbled across the person who killed Stella. The only problem is *he knows* I figured it out, and he made a couple of little innuendos suggesting that I need to be careful or else something bad may happen to my baby."

"That's not an innuendo," Kyle said flatly. "That's a threat."

"Not the way he said it," Jenny replied, once again glancing in the mirror. "It was an insinuation."

"Okay," Kyle began. "Where are you now, and who is this guy?"

"I'm in my car, heading toward Stella's old house so I can be with my husband. I'm going to make a point of not being alone right now."

"Excellent," he replied. "That's good thinking. Now who is the suspect?"

"His name is Leo, and that's all I know. He appears to be in his forties, and his cousin is Ed Pryzbyck." Jenny thought back to the conversation on the deck. "He may or may not have a criminal record. Renee Pryzbyck mentioned something about him falling on hard times, and I believe he was high this afternoon."

Kyle seemed to be jotting down information. "So, what makes you think it was him?"

"He had a tattoo...of a sun...with a scar in the middle that looked like it may have been created by the tip of a fountain pen." She explained her theory about the half-finished letter and the self-defense stabbing. "It occurred to me when I saw it that we may have interpreted Stella's final message incorrectly."

"Okay, well let me get on this right away. If he's threatened you, we need to get him off the street as soon as possible."

"That's what I'm thinking," Jenny said.

"So, here's what I want you to do next, if you haven't done it already," Kyle said, making Jenny feel grateful for the direction. "Call up that connection you have at the police station and see if he can determine if any prints had been lifted from that palm print. Tell him you have been threatened...that will take this old, technically-solved case and put a new sense of urgency on it."

"Got it."

"And Jenny?" His tone turned from professional to personal. "Please be careful."

Jenny looked over her shoulder as she walked up Rob's driveway. Although she knew quite well that Leo had not followed her, nor was he behind her at that moment, she couldn't help but look for him. He had threatened the well-being of her *baby*, and that was unacceptable.

She walked into the unlocked door to find a flurry of activity. Smiling politely at the contractors as she walked past, she eventually found her way to Zack, who was still hard at work in the master bathroom. He was definitely a sight for sore eyes as Jenny approached him, tears forming in her eyes as she slid in for a hug.

"Hey," he said in a surprised tone. "What's the matter?"

She explained the situation to Zack, who held on to her tightly as she spoke. "And now it's just a waiting game," she concluded. "With a potential killer on the loose—who is aware that I'm onto him and is currently in the presence of three innocent people." She buried her head into his shoulder. "This is a nightmare."

"How long will it take in order for them to find out for sure whether or not it was him?"

Jenny let out a deep sigh. "I have no idea."

At that moment, Jenny's phone rang from inside her purse. She immediately let go of Zack's embrace and looked at the caller, excited to see that it was Kyle. "Hey," she said quickly. "Did you find anything?"

"In fact I did," Kyle replied, causing every one of Jenny's nerves to tingle. "His name is Leo Pryzbyck, as it turns out, and he does have quite a colorful criminal background."

Jenny closed her eyes, fearing for what was happening over at Ed and Renee's house at that very moment. "For what?"

"Drug charges, mostly. A few larcenies, and a couple of assaults."

"Nothing more sinister?" Jenny asked.

"Not that he's been caught for, anyway. But I do have one other interesting piece of information."

"What's that?"

"It seems that back in 1988 our friend Mr. Leo Pryzbyck was a resident of the Roseland Apartments."

Jenny was pacing the living room floor when Zack emerged from the back of the house. She flashed him an expression that revealed her despair.

"Still no word?" Zack asked, referring to the phone call Jenny eagerly awaited from Detective Wilks.

"No," Jenny replied grumpily, "and the wait is killing me."

"You do realize that you are probably not the first person he'd call if the prints came back a match," Zack rationalized. "It could be that he's already gotten word that Leo's prints match those at the crime scene, and he's working on a way to get Leo into custody." He put his arm reassuringly around Jenny. "Who knows? He may have Leo in custody already."

With a heavy sigh, Jenny replied, "I just wish I knew what was going on. I have to admit, this guy got under my skin. I realize this isn't the first time my life has been in jeopardy, but this is the first time I've actually been *threatened*. The other times I just found myself in predicaments without realizing I was in danger until it stared me in the face. This time I can see it coming, and it's horrifying."

"What about Orlowski?" Zack asked. "You knew he was a bad guy, and he was out on the street."

Jenny shook her head. "That was different. He wanted to date me; he didn't threaten to hurt me. And secondly, this time I'm carrying a baby. Before I just had to look out for myself...but now that I have a baby's life at stake, it's just all that much more terrifying."

"Well, another difference is that this time we're *married,* and I'm not letting you out of my sight." He looked at her and smiled. "In fact, there's a whole ton of work to be done back there in the bathroom...feel free to throw on some gloves and get cracking. Then I can *really* keep my eye on you."

Making a face, Jenny said, "I think I'll pass, if you don't mind."

With a playful shrug Zack replied, "Suit yourself. But to be clear, I don't think you're pulling your weight around here."

Zack returned to work while Jenny continued her pacing; the constant motion allowed her to burn off some of her nervous energy. After what seemed like an eternity, her phone finally did ring, and the caller was Detective Dante Wilks.

"Detective Wilks," she said eagerly. "Thank you so much for getting back to me."

"No problem," he replied. "But I'm afraid I have to tell you some bad news. I looked into the evidence on the case, and while the forensics team did go through the motions of lifting a print from the door sill, there wasn't a print to be lifted. The blood stain was too smeared to yield any useful evidence."

Jenny hung her head. "So, we're essentially waiting for the DNA analysis to come back to see if Leo is linked to this crime at all?"

"I'm afraid so."

"And that may take a while," Jenny added.

"Indeed it might. In the meantime, you can go to the courthouse and start the process of filing a restraining order against him if you'd like. If he did threaten your well-being, or that of your baby, you can protect yourself in that way."

"But if I get a restraining order, Leo will know it, correct?"

"Of course," Detective Wilks said. "He would need to know the terms."

"Then I'd rather not," Jenny replied. "Then he would know for sure that I'm on to him. I'd rather just pretend I didn't see the connection. I actually think I might be safer that way."

"Okay, well, be careful," Wilks said. "Honestly, this is one of the worst parts of the job...having an idea of who the guy is but being unable to do anything about it."

Jenny nodded slowly. "I'm coming to learn that."

Jenny did little more than pick at her dinner in the hospital cafeteria. With her level of nervousness being what it was, her appetite was non-existent.

Noticing that Jenny was simply stirring her food around with her fork, Zack said, "Steve just told me he's hungry and he wants you to eat a little more of that." He looked at her with a loving smirk.

Jenny lowered her shoulders. "I know. It's just the thought of Ed, Renee and Megan being at that house with Leo...I just can't bring myself to eat."

"Do you really think they're in danger?" Zack put his hand on Jenny's shoulder. "I mean, Leo wouldn't really gain anything by hurting them, would he?"

"No, I guess he wouldn't. And I purposely haven't told them so that they don't act funny around him. As far as Leo is concerned, I'm the only one who has made the connection."

"Exactly," Zack said, gesturing around the large cafeteria "And you're about as safe as you can be in here." He rubbed her back. "Please try to relax. I can tell that you're making yourself sick with worry."

Jenny let out a little laugh. "I guess if I am going to make myself sick, a hospital is the place to do it."

"How about you just don't make yourself sick at all," Zack suggested. He looked around for a moment and noted, "Do you find it just a bit ironic that we're sitting in the same cafeteria that Stella must have sat in a thousand times? Who knows...she may have sat in this very spot a time or two."

Jenny also scanned the room as she remembered the real reason she was still in Georgia—justice for Stella, the young nurse who certainly must have had her share of meals in that very room. "Normally, in a situation like this, I'd be feeling an overwhelming sense of déjà vu," Jenny said. "But this time it isn't Stella who is contacting me...it's Nate, who doesn't have any ties to this hospital other than the surgeries he had when he was little."

Jenny froze for a moment as a thought hit her.

Zack seemed to detect her change in demeanor. "What's happening?" he asked.

She continued to remain still as she pieced her thought together. Reaching for her phone, she announced, "I have to make a call."

"To who?" Zack asked.

She glanced at him as she called up her list of contacts. "Shane Burke."

"Why do you want to call him?"

Jenny pressed the dial button. "Listen and find out." She covered her free ear with her finger to drown out the background noise from the large dinner crowd. When Shane picked up on the other end, she began with, "Doctor Burke? It's Jenny Larrabee...I've been working with Kyle Buchanan on Stella Jorgenson's case."

He didn't sound amused by the call. "What is it?"

She got straight to the point. "I remember you saying that you were at work the afternoon that Stella was killed, is that correct?"

"Yes."

"And by that you mean you were in the emergency room at Saint Mary's Hospital."

"Yes."

Jenny let out a sigh as she gathered her thoughts. "I realize you're bound by doctor-patient confidentiality and all of that, but I also know you said you remember that day clearly because of what happened. So, I'm wondering if you recall seeing a particular patient come in that day with a stab wound."

"A stab wound?"

"Yes...A small stab wound right in the middle of a tattoo of a sun, just below the left collarbone. The cut was made by the tip of a fountain pen and disfigured the face of the tattoo."

The silence on the other end seemed to take forever. "You know what? I do remember that...not because of the strangeness of it—we get a lot of that—but because that's what I was doing on the afternoon Stella was killed. I remember thinking afterward that she should have been in there helping me stitch up that sun. If she had been, there's a good chance she'd still be alive today."

Jenny removed her finger from her ear to give Zack an emphatic thumbs-up. "Doctor Burke, if I put you in touch with a detective, would you be willing to attest to that?"

"Sure. Does this have anything to do with Stella's murder?"

With a smile she said, "It just might. I have reason to believe that the wound to the sun was inflicted by the pen Stella was using to write a letter to her sister when the attack happened. In fact, that was the pen that she earned after five years of service at the hospital."

Shane didn't reply right away. "You mean that guy I stitched up was Stella's killer?"

In her excitement to solve the case, Jenny hadn't considered that notion might have been upsetting to Doctor Burke. With much less vigor in her voice, she said, "That's the impression I'm under."

After another long silence, the doctor replied coldly, "Then I should have used succinylcholine instead of lidocaine."

Jenny paused before saying, "I don't know what that means."

Doctor Burke made it very clear. "Instead of numbing him, it would have killed the bastard."

Jenny sat on the edge of the bed after checking for the third time that the guest bedroom window at the Larrabee's house was locked. "I'm still so worried about Megan and the Pryzbycks…not Leo, of course, but Ed and Renee."

Zack, who was already in bed, rolled over onto his side. "Mumford Springs is a small town. If a murder had happened there today, it would have made the news. I just checked not too long ago, and nothing got reported."

She glanced at the clock. "It's a pretty safe bet that Megan is home by now. Should I just give her a call?"

"If you want," Zack replied.

"But if she is still at the Pryzbyck's, there's a chance Leo will see that I'm calling her. Then I might be putting her into danger that she wasn't in before."

"Then don't call her," Zack said.

Jenny was not amused by the fact that he didn't seem to be taking this seriously. "I feel like their safety is at stake," she said unhappily. "You could show a little more concern."

Zack shrugged, and his voice got a little defensive. "I'm not sure what you want me to say. I told you to call her, and you didn't seem to like that. Now I'm telling you not to, and you don't like that either. What, exactly, can I say that will make you happy?"

She looked at him with sad eyes. "You can tell me that Leo Pryzbyck is behind bars."

Zack's brief animosity appeared to subside, and he patted the bed next to him. Jenny slid into her spot and cuddled up into his shoulder.

"Why don't you call Megan first thing in the morning? I doubt at this age she's having a sleepover, so it should be safe to call her bright and early. Would that make you feel better?"

Jenny sighed and relaxed a little bit. "It will." She began to stroke his chest with her hand. After a few moments of silent cuddling, Jenny added, "And I know of a little something else that will make me feel better, too." She ended the statement with a suggestive giggle.

"Good Lord, woman. I'm not a piece of meat."

Grateful for Zack's ability to always make her laugh, she smiled and replied, "You're not? Then why am I with you?"

"Isn't it obvious?"

"Oh, dear," Jenny said, bracing herself for the undoubtedly egotistical response.

"It's because I get along so well with my dad. Did you see us tonight? We actually had a civil conversation without any sarcasm or insults or *anything*."

"I did see that," Jenny said, "and it was very impressive."

"Although," Zack replied with a furrowed brow, "I'm pretty sure he's still on a high dosage of painkillers. Perhaps tonight's pleasantness was the product of a little drug-induced euphoria."

Jenny rested her chin on Zack's chest. "Honey, why is it you always seem to end up talking about your father when I'm trying to hit on you?"

Zack thought for a moment before saying, "Good point." In one swift motion he rolled over on top of Jenny and began to kiss her.

"Well, at least I know they're still alive," Jenny said as she put on her shirt. "I have plans to meet Megan, Ed and Renee out for breakfast...on the QT, of course."

Zack, who had just returned to the bedroom after taking a shower, kissed her on the cheek. "That's good. See? I told you there was nothing to worry about."

Jenny crinkled her nose. "I wouldn't say *that*. It just turned out well, that's all. So, what's your plan for today?"

"I think we can finish up the bathroom, and then after that we might be done...or at least, *I* might be done. If there are any little details left, I think the guys can handle it."

"So, does that mean we can head back to Tennessee soon? And get far away from Leo Pryzbyck? Is that what you're saying?"

Zack smiled at his wife. "That's exactly what I'm saying. We can leave as soon as tonight if you want."

"You know, I just might want that. I'll have to see how this breakfast goes before I say for sure, but after the way I felt last night, I think I'll just want to get the hell out of Dodge."

"I kind of want to get out of here, too. I want you safe, obviously, but my dad is also checking out of the hospital today, and he doesn't need to come home to a house full of company. I'll help my mom set up a bed for him downstairs, and then after that I think we should get out of their hair."

"I agree. Your dad won't want an audience."

Zack let out a sheepish smile. "There's actually another reason I want to be home, too...I miss Baxter."

Jenny laughed. "You're a big sap, you know that?"

"Hey, you don't want to mess with the bond between a man and his dog."

She patted him on the chest. "Well, why don't you go get started on that bathroom, I'll go have breakfast, and we'll see if we can't get you playing fetch by bedtime."

Jenny felt relief when she saw Megan, Ed and Renee in the lobby of the restaurant. Although she hadn't yet shared her concerns with them, she greeted each of them with a hug, delighted that her decision to leave early yesterday hadn't cost any of them their well-being. They all probably thought she was just being over-friendly, but she didn't care. They were alive, and that was all she needed.

Once they got seated, nervousness rose within Jenny. She realized she was about to tell Ed that his cousin had most likely committed a murder; this was not going to be an easy conversation to have, especially considering he and Renee would have to go back to their house that they currently shared with Leo after breakfast was over.

Jenny clasped her hands together at the table, sucking in a deep breath before speaking. "I'm so glad you all could come out here this morning," she began. "I think I may have made a break in the case."

"Oh my God," Megan said, putting her hand over her mouth. "Was it my cousin?"

Shaking her head, Jenny replied, "As it turns out, no." She gathered herself for a moment and said with a wince, "Ed, I actually think it was *your* cousin."

He looked shocked. "*My* cousin? You mean Leo?"

Jenny nodded solemnly. "I'm afraid so."

"I didn't even know he was a suspect," Ed proclaimed.

"Neither did I, until yesterday." Jenny explained the connection about the sun. "It wasn't until I saw his disfigured tattoo that I realized I may have been misinterpreting Stella's message all along. The scary part is I think he saw me eyeing his tattoo, and he may know that I'm on to him."

"Oh my God," Renee exclaimed as she turned to Ed. "So, it *wasn't* because he overheard me yesterday."

Confused, Jenny asked, "What are you talking about."

"Oh my God," Renee said again, causing Jenny to become frightened.

Ed sighed before he began, "When we woke up this morning, Leo's car wasn't in the driveway. When we looked into his room, we noticed it was empty."

"Empty?" Jenny cried.

"I'm afraid so," Ed said with a reluctant nod. Glancing up at Jenny, he added, "It appears your new prime suspect may have skipped town."

Chapter 19

Jenny felt her heart practically beat out of her chest. "He *left*?"

Renee's expression showed she was just as unsettled as Jenny. "I thought it was because he had overheard me saying I wanted him gone, but I guess he left because he knew he'd been found out."

Ed shook his head and raised his hand. "I'm not defending my cousin in any way...but do you know for sure it was him?"

"As sure as I can be. Ironically, Leo got his stab wound stitched up at the hospital where Stella worked." Jenny looked at Megan, who would understand the significance. "It turns out Doctor Burke was the one who had worked on him. He remembered that case because it was what he was doing when Stella got killed...just like you all remember you had spent that afternoon watching *Rainman*." She turned back to face Ed. "I think it would be a little too much of a coincidence that Leo happened to get an injury to his *sun* at the same time Stella was killed. Especially since a bloody handprint was found on the back door...the back door that led to the apartments where Leo lived at the time."

Megan shook her head. "But I don't get it. What motive would he have had? We had never even met Leo."

Ed closed his eyes, looking as if he might be sick. "Oh, God. I think I can answer that."

The others waited for him to elaborate.

He hung his head in shame before saying, "After that cookout we had at Megan and Stella's the weekend before, I remember telling my cousin that Stella had slept with two different guys in the same day. I made some kind of crass comment that if ever he wanted to, *you know*..." He covered his face with his hands, wiping them down to his chin. He sighed and continued. "...he probably could do it if he paid that house a visit." He quickly held up his hands. "But I was just kidding... I never thought in a million years he'd actually *go* there, let alone harm her in any way." Ed looked sick again. "I can't believe I played a hand in this. I feel positively awful."

"Nobody's blaming you," Jenny assured him. "Every young guy has made crass comments at some point in his life...in no way does that make you even remotely responsible for what happened to her."

Ed ran his fingers through his hair. "But why would I say something like that to a guy with a drug habit? That was just stupid."

Jenny looked at Ed. "What kind of drugs did he do?"

"Back then? PCP."

"I don't know what that would do," Jenny admitted. "Would that potentially cause him to commit murder?"

Ed nodded. "Absolutely. It's known for inducing mood swings and hallucinations. He would have been capable of anything if he was having a bad trip."

Megan looked at Ed. "Do you happen to know if Leo used to have a switch blade?"

He once again looked like he could be ill. With sunken shoulders, he announced, "He carried one with him at all times. Was that the murder weapon?"

With a nod, Megan said, "Afraid so. And I don't remember us having one at the house, so the killer must have brought it with him."

Ed closed his eyes. "That sounds about right. Like I said, he never left home without it."

Turning to Jenny, Renee asked, "Do the authorities know about this? We need to let them know that Leo is gone. The sooner they can start looking for him, the less of a head start he will have."

Jenny reached into her purse for her phone. As she searched for Dante Wilks' phone number, she glanced up at Ed and posed, "Do you have any idea where he may have gone?"

Ed thought for a moment and shook his head. "Not off the top of my head. Nothing strikes me as obvious."

Jenny pressed the button to call the detective. "Wilks," he said when he picked up.

"Hi, detective Wilks, It's Jenny Larrabee again. I need to talk to you about Leo Pryzbyck."

"Uh oh," Wilks said. "He didn't carry through on his threats, did he?"

"No, it's nothing like that," Jenny said, "but it appears he did skip town."

"He skipped town?"

"Afraid so." Jenny explained the revelations that had come to light over the past few minutes. "And did you get a call from Doctor Burke last night?"

"I did," Detective Wilks replied. "Well, it looks to me like we may be on to something here. I think at this point it might be worth officially re-opening the case and taking a long, hard look a certain Mr. Leo Pryzbyck."

Jenny was as relieved as she could be under the circumstances. "Thank you so much, detective. This will mean a lot to both Stella's family and the Minnicks."

Wilks' tone was serious. "It'll mean even more if we can get him into custody."

Jenny drove straight to Rob's house after breakfast, finding Zack having a conversation with Willy in the Sanders' driveway as she pulled up. When she got out of the car, Zack greeted her with a huge smile, announcing, "And there she is."

"Were your ears burning?" Willy asked.

With an apprehensive smile, Jenny asked, "No...should they have been?"

"Well, we were just talking about you. I was telling Zack, here, that Rob wanted me to take a picture of the two of you for his wall. I'm sure you noticed the *hall of fame* he had going on in there."

"The hall of fame," Jenny repeated with a laugh. "Is that what he calls it?"

"Yup," Willy confirmed. "Sure is."

Once Jenny got past the name, she realized the implications of the request. "He really wants a picture of me and Zack on his wall?"

"You've changed his life," Willy said, "and he wants to remember you."

Zack chimed in, "He also wants us to see if we can get a picture of Nate from the Minnicks. He believes that Nate is that guardian angel he's been talking about for years, and he wants him on the wall, too."

Jenny placed her hand on her heart as she felt breathless for a moment. Nate had gone from being regarded as a villain to being seen as a guardian angel; she felt like her mission in Mumford Springs was complete.

"I'll see what I can do," Jenny said. "Lord knows Nate's mother had no shortage of pictures of him." Turning to Willy, she added, "Did you hear that we may have gotten the case solved?"

"That's what Zack was saying. It was someone who lived in the apartments?"

"It looks that way," Jenny replied. "And now, apparently, he's skipped town."

"Skipped town?" Zack asked with dismay.

Jenny explained the story, adding, "And that's one more reason why I want to get the hell out of here."

"He's probably long gone by now," Willy reasoned. "I bet he's more concerned with staying one step ahead of the law than he is with getting revenge on you."

"I hope you're right," Jenny said. "But it will still be hard to sleep at night with him out there."

"Had I known they had the wrong person in jail back in '88, I wouldn't have slept for decades," Willy replied. "I had five kids running around this cul-de-sac...and a lunatic living a few hundred yards away. You can even *see* the apartments from here in the winter time."

Guilt surged through Jenny's veins; she felt it would only be alleviated through honesty. "Willy, I do have a confession to make. I did have an investigation into Marcus going on."

"Marcus?"

Jenny sighed. "I didn't think it was him, but since Stella's last words were to look for the son, I had to consider every possibility."

"Well, I could have told you it wasn't him right off the bat. He wasn't even around that weekend. He was at baseball camp in Kentucky."

"Wow," Jenny said. "You have a great memory if you can remember that."

Willy laughed. "I was getting ready to mow the lawn when I saw Nate running out of the house. Now, why would I be mowing my own lawn if I had a seventeen-year-old son at home? I raised my kids better than that."

"I'm sure you did," Jenny said with a smile. "I'm sure you did."

Three weeks later

Jenny sat at the kitchen table of her mother's downstairs apartment. "The DNA came back a match," she told Isabelle. "Now they know for sure it was Leo."

A look of worry gripped Isabelle's face. "Is he still on the lam?"

There was something funny about hearing her mother say *on the lam*. "Afraid so. But now there's an official APB for him, so they should be able to find him." Jenny's words were designed to comfort her mother; she only wished she could believe them herself.

"You said he only had a few hundred dollars to his name when he disappeared," Isabelle noted. "How long can he stay in hiding with just that much money?"

"Unfortunately, criminals don't need their own money. He will just use someone else's."

At that point, Jenny's phone rang with a number she didn't recognize. "I'm going to get this, ma. I don't know what it's about." She stood up from the table and took a few steps into the living room. "Hello?"

"Hello, my name is Andrew Parker; I'm looking for Jenny Watkins-Larrabee."

Jenny was curious who this stranger could have been if he knew both her previous and current names. "This is."

"Miss Watkins-Larrabee, I don't know if you remember me, but I am the lawyer representing Elanor Whitby's estate."

Now that he said that, she did recall the name. "Oh, yes, hi Mr. Parker."

Although, now she was even more curious about the reason for the call.

"Well, I'm pleased to inform you that Ms. Whitby had set up a trust."

"A trust?"

"Yes. While she'd left you a sizable chunk of her estate, she did keep some of it set aside with the instructions that you were to get the money when one of two things happened: either ten years passed, or your divorce became final. I've been checking periodically, and I see you not only have gotten divorced, but you've been remarried. Congratulations."

His words stopped having meaning as she tried to contemplate what was being said. "Wait a minute. Elanor had *more* money set aside that I would only get *after* my divorce?"

The lawyer laughed. "It seems Ms. Whitby didn't have too much affinity for your ex-husband. She wanted to make sure that you would receive some money that he couldn't touch in the event of a divorce. Or, she figured, if you survived another ten years as a married couple, that meant you had ironed out your differences and you were presumably happy with him."

The shock wore off just enough for Jenny to laugh out loud. "That woman was a genius."

"You don't reach her level of success without a good deal of intelligence."

"Indeed you don't," Jenny replied. "Okay, so just how much money are we talking?"

"What you had received was two-thirds of her estate. The other third is sitting in the trust, waiting for you to claim it."

Having been a teacher, Jenny knew her fractions. "Wait a minute...a *third?* That means I'm getting back the same amount that my ex-husband just took."

She could tell Mr. Parker was smiling when he said, "It's as if your ex-husband never got a dime."

The July air felt heavy around Jenny as she sat next to the birdhouse that hung in her backyard. Yellowed pine needles stuck out of the hole, evidence that the family of Chickadees was making itself comfortable in their new home. "You are a very cunning woman," Jenny said out loud as she waved her finger. "I still have so much to learn from you."

Jenny paused as if waiting for a response.

With a sigh, she glanced over at the birdhouse. "I'm so happy to have you back here, where you belong. I'm sorry about the way Greg treated you." A sinister smile graced Jenny's lips as she added, "Although, I guess you got the last laugh on that one, didn't you?"

Once again Jenny grew quiet, Elanor's absence made painfully clear by the silence. "I wish there was a way I could repay you for everything you've done for me." Jenny smirked and added, "Although, I know you would say that I already have just by using the money to help people. Even Zack is into it...you should see what he did to Rob Denton's house."

Jenny stopped her speech once again, but this time for a different reason. "Hang on," she said. "I'll be back." She smiled and shot a parting glance at the birdhouse before darting back inside. She headed for the small tribute she'd created for Elanor and Steve, carefully removing the only photograph she had of Elanor from its frame. She studied the image for a moment, smiling at the woman who went on to touch so many lives, even long after her own was over.

She really did miss Elanor.

Remembering her mission, she headed straight for her scanner, placing the picture of Elanor on the screen and saving it into her computer. After a few keystrokes she began an email to Rob, simply entitled:

For your hall of fame.

To be continued in Possessed.